DARK
THERMOPYLAE

Belinda Harrison

ISBN-13: 978-0-6483721-9-6 (US/EUR Paperback)
Published by Gee Be Publications

DEDICATION

For Skylar and Alexis who have shared the inside of my head with important data I use to keep me alive and less important (but extremely funny) dad jokes. You've become more than just a couple of girls I think about before I fall asleep and more than conversation starters at parties – you've given me somewhere to go when the real world seems too overwhelming and for that I thank you (well I would if you weren't figments of my imagination)

1

"Her power grows, Skylar, can you not feel it?"

"She is not who you think she is." It was my voice answering Ares, but I saw the two of us as though I was outside my body.

Low-burning torches around the room illuminated a shining floor and black marble walls and I knew where I was; Ares' palace at Olympos.

I had been there only once before, ten winters ago. Before Ava was born. Before we learnt that I was not the Chosen One as Ares had believed. As I had believed.

"We both know that is not the truth. She may only be almost nine winters old but her power grows. I feel it through every part of my being. It is even hotter and sweeter than what I felt when *your* power began to emerge. It is almost time," Ares grinned.

"She is too young. You said it yourself; she is not even nine winters old yet. It is too soon."

"No. We shall see each other again before long," he laughed. A blinding light flashed and I turned my head, the echo of Ares' laugh remaining long after he disappeared.

2
SKYLAR
16th moon full, Moon of Thargelion, 500BC

I woke with a start, my skin covered in sweat where Alexis' arm lay across my stomach. I carefully removed her limb and pushed back the covers, pulling on my tunic before crossing to the door and slipping through. The central chamber and palace beyond were dark but I stepped the few paces across to Ava's room, as I had so many times since she had arrived, without needing a light to guide me.

When she was a baby, I had always answered her cries in the night, knowing how much Alexis had to do during the days and nights when I was away with the army. Lately that had been more often than I would have preferred and the responsibility for our daughter would once again fall to my wife when I journeyed with my father and Nasrin to Naxos in a week's time.

Moeris and I commanded the army of Trachis equally. Moeris oversaw the men from his position within the barracks, whereas I led them from the palace, joining them for training every day and remaining with them when our duty took us from home. After what had happened with Ares and the Keres, I was not comfortable leaving Alexis and Ava for long periods of time. When we journeyed to battle I always returned to Trachis ahead of the main army. Moeris and the other men accepted it without question; they knew my first priority was to the royal family, as it had been since I first arrived. They followed Moeris' instruction in my absence without hesitation for he was a fair and well-respected leader and they had known him far longer than me.

I pushed open the wood and leant against the doorframe. Ava's long hair was the same dark shade as my own and lay across her forehead and down her back, straight and thick. I watched the gentle rise and fall of her small, sun-kissed shoulders; their color highlighting the many candlemarks she spent at the hot springs near our home. She murmured several unintelligible words, no doubt finding herself in Morpheus' realm behind her closed eyes.

Much had changed since I decided to stay and begin a life with Alexis in Trachis – the small child before me for one. My daughter. Alexis' daughter. Our precious child. Ava; Princess of Thermopylae and heir to the throne at Trachis once Alexis and I found ourselves in the Underworld.

I smiled. The words *my daughter* were not two I ever believed I would use for myself before I arrived in the region of Thermopylae. Then again, I never expected to fall in love and want to remain in one place for the rest of my days either. I was not seeking love or a partner. I did not believe I deserved or needed it, and yet love found me anyway and showed me how wrong I was.

Thaddeus' blood flows within Ava as well of course. In that respect, she is as much his daughter as she is ours, not that she knows of their bond. He has always behaved as a fond uncle, treating her as his favored niece, rather than a father. She adores him in return. For a time, I worried that Thaddeus would attempt to act as her parent too, but he never has, allowing Alexis and I to parent her as we see fit in all matters related to her upbringing and happiness, just as he does for his own children with Hesper.

Alexis and Hesper have remained close, enjoying bringing up their children together. When Eumelia and Ava were born, Nikomachos, Pamphilos and Tritonos fussed over them both, and the girls have grown with the fighting and fierce protection of older brothers. With Ava's birth upon us earlier than expected due to the line of the Keres, I had wondered if she would continue to age faster than Eumelia and the other children her age. I had questioned Ares on it but he did not know and as the days passed, Alexis and I were relieved to find that she grew as expected, rather than influenced by a line I hoped she bore no resemblance to. That fact aided to strengthen our belief that Ares was wrong about who she might be.

I was not the only one to have become a parent since coming to Trachis; my faithful stallion, Skotos, had also fathered a son, and Philo was now Ava's loyal companion. When I first raised the idea of a horse for Ava with Alexis, I had expected her to offer Calla for the task, but Calla was well past her foal rearing days, so instead I travelled to the rich breeding grounds of Larissa to search for a suitable mare. My father was considering a horse for Nasrin as well, so the two of us went together, choosing Raisa for both. She was a brilliant choice, gentle in nature and yet spirited enough when it suited her. It was not long after Raisa and Skotos were introduced, that they produced the healthy bronze foal, just in time for Ava's fourth birthing day celebration.

Agrias and Melina still ruled Trachis, though they had told us if Alexis and I wanted to begin our reign before one of them passed, they would stand aside, giving guidance in any matters we asked for. Perhaps one day we would accept the offer but for now both of us were content to have them remain as rulers.

Father and Nasrin still lived with Melina's parents in town, Ophelos and my father overseeing the crafting of our weapons and coins, and sale of the same. The two men had become firm friends, just as my father and Agrias had when we first arrived in Trachis more than ten winters ago.

Nasrin and Melina had also grown close – akin now to sisters. They fussed over Ava as proud grandmothers do, taking her to the agora with them at least once a week.

I blew out a deep breath, noting how small Ava still appeared in the large bed I had once shared with Alexis. She would soon be seen as a young woman, offers for betrothal having already arrived from a number of interested parties. We had settled on none, nor did we intend to for quite a while yet. There would be time for that.

Time.

The words from my dream echoed through my mind and a shiver of fear skittered down my back and settled itself in my stomach. I wanted to believe that the dreams I had had of Ares, of what he had told me tonight did not mean anything. But they were becoming too frequent, and he was too insistent that the time when he returned was near. Though Ava had displayed no desire for cruelty or unusual talents, how could we truly know? My own ability to use the amulet and easily discard those I loved had not emerged until I was in my twentieth winter; but to be fair, that was only after Ares decided I was ready.

I had convinced myself that Ares had been wrong that my daughter was the one he had waited so long for and Alexis and I had not spoken of the God of War, or what he promised Ava would be, for many winters. There had been no need. But now … now I was not so certain.

I reached to my neck, fingering the amulet that hung there. I still wore it, mainly so I knew where it was should Ares return. Alexis had long ago persuaded me to keep it close as it was the only connection I still had to my mother, and she believed it special for that reason alone. I knew she was afraid of it. To most people it appeared to be a unique piece of jewelry, but she and I knew it was capable of far more. I had never been tempted to attempt to use it again, and it had always remained dark and innocent. Well, except for that once …

We lost Calla that day. And Tritonos.

I was at the training arena between the Melas and Dyras Rivers, almost done for the day. As they had so often, Ava, Tritonos, Nikomachos and Lysistratos had taken Ava's colt, Philo, to practice jumps and such in the open grassy space between the barracks and the Melas River. Ava was six-and-a-half-winters old and had just begun riding Philo, the two of them having already formed a strong bond and immense trust in the preceding two winters, when Philo was still too young to carry her. Alexis' mare, Calla, was quite old by then, and given Tritonos' simple nature, she was the only horse anyone permitted him to ride when he insisted he wished to. The older boys were in charge of the younger two, and Nikomachos enjoyed the role of horse trainer on such afternoons.

Ava and Philo were at one end of the grass, Tritonos and Calla trotting merrily at the other. Calla disturbed a brown horned viper, encouraged out early by the unusual spring heat. The snake bit Calla on her lower leg. She reared up and Tritonos was thrown from her back. He fell to the ground, knocked unconscious until the old mare's hoof crashed down on his head, ensuring he never woke again. Calla took off but she did not get far before the poison stopped her own heart and she fell to the ground, dead.

The two boys and Ava rushed over, Ava and Philo arriving first at Tritonos' side. Unfortunately, the viper was still nearby and raised itself to attack again. Philo threw up his hooves in defense, dislodging Ava in the process and leaping over the prone figure as he took off towards the barracks.

I had felt the heat of the amulet before I saw the orange rays peek out from my cuirass and instantly knew I had to find Ava; that she was in danger. I left the soldiers and ran, sword in hand, meeting Nikomachos at the Dyras River. He told me what had happened as we raced toward them. I barely paused as I slashed at the head of the snake, poised once again on its tail above Lysistratos, who was on his hands and knees shielding Ava from the hissing creature. I dropped to my knees beside the boy, my eyes immediately finding my daughter's closed ones. Lysistratos assured me it was just from the bump on her head – which he quickly pointed out – and I nodded gratefully as he drew back from her. I could tell from the angle of Ava's arm and leg that the bones were broken and I briefly considered pulling out the amulet and holding it above her. I was not certain I could even do anything with it, but more than that, I left it where it was because I feared what I might accidently do to her if it still denied me what I wanted when I attempted to use it.

I had scooped Ava up, Nikomachos gathering Tritonos' lifeless body and Lysistratos bringing my sword. The four of us raced back to the palace; shock, fear and adrenaline propelling our shaking limbs on.

The devastation and guilt at Tritonos' death ran deep through Ava and the boys, each believing they should have done more, or insisted Tritonos remain closer to them. But I, along with the other adults, knew there was nothing more they could have done. How could they have known what was to happen that day? How many times had they been there, doing the same thing? How many more days after Ava recovered did they practice in the grass with friend and horse?

I too felt guilt at Tritonos' passing, mostly because I was so grateful that Ava survived relatively unscathed, other than the moon of inactive healing she had to go through. I recalled how frustrating it was to have to remain still when you were used to being so active and had done my best to entertain her while her wounds healed.

I never told anyone about the amulet's behavior that day – attempting to convince myself it was just a coincidence, or a trick of the light. But lately, with the recurring dreams of Ares, I had begun to wonder if it was the protection part of the hematite which had alerted me to Ava's danger then. I did not want to believe that to be true. If it was, then it would mean that for all I had insisted that Ava was free of the Ker blood, the amulet knew better. Ares may speak true about the power she held within her. And that frightened me more than anything else.

I felt the warm presence behind me before Alexis' hand touched the small of my back. "Skylar? Is everything well?" she murmured.

I raised my arm and she ducked underneath, wrapping hers around my waist as I placed a kiss on the top of her head. "Yes. I had a nightmare and wanted to check on Ava." She nodded and squeezed me tighter. She did not press me on the content, no doubt believing that I continued to re-live the night she birthed Ava; for almost a winter after Ares and Grandmother Dianthe left Trachis, I spent much of my sleep in fitful recollection. I had almost died, almost missed a life with Alexis and Ava. Were it not for the deep love Alexis had for me, and I for her in return, I probably would have. I was in no doubt of that.

But just as I had never shared with Alexis what had happened with the amulet the day Ava was injured, neither had I told her of the dreams of Ares I had been having. I would eventually, but for now, I would not worry her unnecessarily.

Alexis' eyes found our sleeping child before she turned back to me, her voice barely above a whisper, but full of certainty as she grinned. "I believe I know a way to make you forget all about that dream."

"Oh?" I asked, raising an eyebrow.

"Absolutely," she assured me, taking her arms from my waist and sliding her fingers through mine instead. She pulled gently and I grasped the door handle, closing it quietly behind us as I allowed Alexis to lead me back to our room.

Once inside, she turned, ridding me of my tunic and sliding her naked body against mine. "Come back to bed and I shall replace your haunted dreams with far more pleasant desires." I smiled in reply, barely having time to do so before she claimed my lips fiercely.

Much may have changed since I arrived in Trachis, but the one aspect which had not was how much I still wanted Alexis. I still desired her, needed her, with the same intensity and the same love and lust I had felt ever since I woke in the palace to her gentle caresses all those winters ago. And I knew she felt the same for me in return.

3

4 moons later
2nd waning, Moon of Boedromion, 499BC

The boat rocked gently beneath my sandaled feet. The sweet tang of the ginger slice between my teeth effectively prevented my stomach from returning my last meal to the water around us and I was grateful Gnosidicus had been able to procure some of the root on such short notice – and that it was working against the sickness the rolling waves caused.

I could barely make them out in the soft moonlight, but my father and Nasrin sat nearby, waiting for Nasrin's friend – Megabates – to reach us. We kept the torches extinguished so as not to call attention to ourselves, and spoke only sparingly in hushed tones.

Megabates was cousin to Darius, King of Persia – a man who was not only the father of Nasrin's eldest and youngest children, but her most hated of enemies. Fortunately, Megabates held no love for his kin and had been devastated when the future King of Persia bragged to him that he had raped the Babylonian girl when her father refused to sell her to him. Megabates and Darius had both been in Babylon that winter and for Megabates, his love for Nasrin blossomed the moment he saw her. That was before they had even spoken and before Darius defiled her, ensuring Nasrin's hatred for their family was entrenched in every fiber of her being, and giving Megabates no chance to charm her himself.

When Darius eventually succeeded in taking Nasrin to Persia, Megabates had requested charge of her and her daughter in an attempt to right the wrong against her. It was Megabates' highest duty to ensure Nasrin and her children were safe whenever the royal family moved homes from Pāsārgād to Susa or Babylon in the winter, and to see them safely to and from any other destination Darius requested they travel to.

For many moons, Nasrin did not trust the apparent kindness of Megabates, but eventually Democedes, the Greek healer who also found himself imprisoned in Susa, convinced her to trust the man. It was Megabates who spread the rumor of Nasrin's death among those in the royal palace when she fled the city, and he who organized Nasrin and Ava's safe passage from Miletus to Greece.

Many, including Darius himself, believed that his rule was untouchable. But there was, and always had been, those who worked against their king from the very heart of his circle of confidants without his knowledge. If Darius ever found out, his punishment would no doubt be swift and harsh, though he appeared so preoccupied with conquering the lands he wanted that he gave no thought to threats closer to home.

Before my father and I agreed to aid in Naxos, Nasrin had never told me of Megabates' assistance in her escape; only that of Democedes. It was not that she did not trust me with the information, but rather that she still feared Darius and she wanted to protect all of us from him. After Megabates' messenger arrived and we began travelling to the south-east, she spoke of it fully with my father and me. It sought to reinforce our decision to join the Naxians in defending their home.

Megabates wanted our allies – the Macedonians and Spartans – to join us in Naxos as well, but Nasrin made it clear to her old friend that the three of us were there only as a personal favor for his help in freeing her from Darius. Apart from the proof we now had that the presence of Spartan or Macedonian warriors were unnecessary in securing victory in Naxos, Nasrin did not want to have Darius' interest in the other powerful Greek cities peaked if word reached him that they were there. I doubted my friend, King Cleomenes, in Sparta or Agrias' brother, Amyntas, in Macedonia would wish for the same.

Within half-a-candlemark, the gentle waves lapping against the side of our vessel began to splash over and wet our feet, the distinct sound of slapping oars reaching us.

"Someone approaches," Father murmured, though there was no reason to voice such an obvious statement.

"Nasrin?" a voice enquired from the darkness to our right.

"Megabates هسـ تـ يم، ايـ نجا ما" she replied in their native tongue – telling us she had said *we are here, Megabates.*

The Persian General's face appeared a moment later when the man beside him struck two pieces of flint together. The head of their torch only highlighted their faces so my father lit his, effectively illuminating the entirety of our small party.

Though his next words were foreign to me, I did not need to understand them to see Megabates still held much affection for the woman who now warmed my father's bed.

Nasrin translated the rest of their conversation for Father and me, repeating our questions when we asked them and giving us Megabates' answers.

"I was pleased to receive your message and know you had survived the siege unscathed. It is good to see you again."

"And you," Nasrin nodded. "We understand the Persian fleet is set to return home, defeated, in the morning."

"Indeed. Aristagoras of Miletus shall return in disgrace, and owing much coin to my father and cousins," Megabates replied.

"Your father is Pharnaces of Phrygia, brother to Hystaspes who is King Darius' father, is that true?" my father asked. Megabates nodded.

"Phrygia was once home to King Tantalus, was it not?" I added.

"Yes, before he incurred the wrath of the Gods and found himself in Tartarus it was," Megabates replied. "There have been many well-known Kings of Phrygia. I am certain you have heard of King Midas?"

It was my turn to nod. "Of course. Everything he touched turned to gold, it made him very wealthy … but allow us to focus on why we are here." Megabates inclined his head in reply.

"Are you certain Aristagoras has no knowledge of your involvement in warning the Naxians?" Nasrin asked.

"He has suspicions perhaps but cannot prove his claims so speaks of them to no one," Megabates replied with a shake of his head.

"Are you concerned with Aristagoras' debt to your kin? That your own position and comfortable lifestyle shall be impeded with such coin owed?" I asked.

Megabates shook his head. "I do not rely on my father's position, or my closeness in kinship to the king to be comfortable. I have always made my own coin."

I nodded in acknowledgment and fell silent again.

"I cannot thank you enough for assisting me in ensuring my cousin's kingdom did not reach the islands of the Cyclades," Megabates said.

"The only thanks necessary is to never speak of our involvement. I do not wish to arouse Darius' further interest in our lands," Nasrin replied.

"You mean Greece when you say *your* land?"

"Yes."

"What about Babylon? You do not consider it to be your home?"

"No. It has not been so for many winters. My loyalty, along with my heart, belongs to the Greeks."

"I see," Megabates murmured. His gaze drifted briefly across to my father and my hand tightened against the pommel of my sword; I knew only too well that men and women were capable of killing without hesitation to claim what they wanted – be it land or person.

Nasrin rested her hand on my arm as she spoke again. "We cannot control who we fall in love with."

"We cannot," Megabates agreed. "I shall never speak of your aid here and hope your days are long and happy for all the ones which remain for you."

"Thank you," Nasrin nodded.

"Your lover is most fortunate to call you his. Ensure he treats you well and with the respect you have always deserved." The two men locked gazes, a tense moment passing before they nodded to one another in agreement.

Megabates spoke again and Nasrin swayed suddenly, my father holding her in place so she did not topple sideways. "What is it? What did he say?" he asked.

Nasrin took a deep breath before she replied. "He said my sons are in Persis, at the palace of Darius." She squared her shoulders and looked to Megabates again. "Are you able to get them out? Does Darius know who they are to him?"

"He does not know, but I cannot remove them. They are there of their own choice. I have spoken briefly with the younger one – Artabanus – asking how he found himself there and where his family is. He says he hails from Verkâna and wishes to serve the Great King, but I have seen him and Aspamitres, who hides himself inside the palace as a eunuch, in secret meetings where normally their paths should not cross."

"You must convince them to leave or, at the very least, find out why they are truly there."

"I shall do my best and send word with what I learn."

"Thank you."

"We should return to the ship before our absence is noted," the man beside Megabates noted.

"Yes," Megabates agreed. "Safe travels to you all."

"And to you," Nasrin nodded.

The soldier with Megabates handed the torch to his General and pushed off our boat, his oars splashing into the darkness below, their light fading as they drifted away.

"It is time we found our way back to those who are eagerly awaiting our return also," my father said, slipping his torch into a notch at the bow of the boat and lowering his own paddle into the water.

"The sooner we find ourselves back in Trachis, the better," I agreed.

We had been away from Trachis for over four moons, the longest Alexis and I had been apart since we met, and I was eager to return to her, and to Ava.

*

Just after dawn two days later, I woke to Nasrin and my father's quiet conversation. I watched the clear blue of the sky above and noted the still-low position of the sun. I was surprised to find myself growing accustomed to the strange movements of the boat. It was only the third time I had ridden in one but I had gone from losing my balance, and the contents of my stomach, on the first morning, to actually being lulled to sleep when I lay down on the hard wooden seats. Though I was not eager to travel in such a manner often, I found I enjoyed it well enough with help from the ginger.

"He still holds favor for you," Father's voice was quiet, but the gentle breeze carried his words to me.

"I wondered when you were going to mention Megabates," Nasrin replied. "You have been quiet since he left."

"Mmm."

Nasrin caught my eye and I rolled mine, which earned me a grin. The two of us had previously spoken of my father's insecurity and oft-noted disbelief that Nasrin still wanted to be with him after indirectly causing her daughter's death winters before. In a way, I knew how he felt – sometimes I found it hard to believe that I had won the affections of a princess and been welcomed so quickly and warmly into her family and circle of friends.

"How he feels is of no importance to me. As I told you before we left Trachis I held no desire for him when I was in Persia. Seeing him again now has not changed that." She leaned across and placed a kiss on Father's cheek. "My heart belongs to you and to you alone."

"Alright. Good," Father mumbled.

"It is. Now, are you going to spend all morning pouting, or are you going to help me row, for I am eager to get home and be alone with you," she teased, not bothering to lower her voice.

"I am well rested, how about *I* row for a while instead?" I laughed, stretching out my arms and legs before sitting up and taking the oar from my father.

"As you wish," he shrugged, allowing me to take the paddles. "If you do not tire too quickly, we should be back in Delphinium before the new day begins at sundown."

I nodded in reply as he lay his long frame across the seats and closed his eyes, Nasrin shooting me another grin as I pulled strongly on the oars and propelled us towards the land. Towards home.

4

We arrived at the harbor of Delphinium at sundown and joined the fishermen and traders returning home from their days – or moons – away, guiding our vessel into the mouth of the Asopos River. We gathered our few belongings from the boat and waved our goodbyes; the fishermen heading towards Oropus, and us for the small home with its stables and sheep yards up the road.

The harbor belonged to the small town of Oropus, which was almost eleven stadia south and inland of where we were. Oropus was on the border of Boeotia and Attica and for as long as anyone could remember, the two states had always claimed that the small town belonged to them. Now, as it often had been, it belonged to Athens, possibly because of the strength and quick anger of the army housed in the great city a hundred and ninety-three stadia away.

On our arrival in Oropus, the path between the town and the harbor had been covered in larkspur – the stems standing tall and proudly displaying their blue flowers. Nasrin had fallen in love with the blooms, but they were long finished now, and the road looked much poorer without their brilliant color. As we approached the house, three children ran up to meet us, calling for their father as they arrived. The younger two took each of Nasrin's hands, the eldest staring up in awe at my father.

A man emerged, wiping his hands on his dirty chiton, and I noticed the youngest of his brood was not with them. "By the gods! I did not believe we would see you again, or my small boat," he laughed, offering his arm.

"You had such little faith in our return, Archippos? I am almost offended," Father smiled, taking Archippos' outstretched arm with one hand and clapping him hard on the back with his other.

"Is Skotos in the stables?" I asked.

"He is. He shall be glad to see you again," Archippos replied with a nod. "My children have taken good care of all three horses since you left. They have grown especially fond of the chestnut stallion you called Skaris."

"He is a fine specimen indeed, has been ever since I purchased him," Father said.

I inclined my head to Archippos and excused myself, making my way to the impressive wooden structure. We had left Skotos, Skaris and Raisa with Archippos in exchange for borrowing his boat to get us to Naxos and back, and just as it was the longest amount of time Alexis and I had been apart, so too it was for Skotos and me in the twenty-odd winters since I had tamed him. Though I had known I would miss him, I had not been overly concerned for his health or wellbeing in my absence; Archippos had spoken of the many horses he had been entrusted with over the winters, and the three animals appeared comfortable in his presence, as well as that of his children before we left.

When I arrived at the second pen, I almost did not recognize my old friend. It appeared Archippos and his children had indeed taken good care of Skotos – so much so that he had grown round from plenty of food and not enough exercise.

"I see you have not missed many meals since we last saw one another," I grinned.

My dark bay stallion whinnied in response, snuffling his warm breath into my ear and lifting my hair. At sixteen-and-a-half-hands high, he was a large beast, though Skaris was almost eighteen – and needed to be – given my father's stature of seven foot. I scratched the off-white patch of hair between his eyes and looked around for Skaris. He was in the pen two down from Skotos, and did not appear to be fairing much better than my own steed with his newly-found girth.

A small girl – Archippos' youngest I realized – stood brushing Father's horse, her head barely reaching the bottom of the stomach she was stroking. Every second or third stroke, Skaris would lower his head to hers and affectionately blow into her hair, causing the young one to giggle hysterically before returning to her task. I grinned, recognizing it as a game Skaris used to play with Thaddeus and Hesper's youngest son Tritonos when he visited him at the stables.

Before Father and I had arrived in Trachis, neither of our horses were used to children, though they had been given plenty of opportunities to become accustomed to the tiny adults since. Nikomachos and Pamphilos often fought over who would be the first to brush our steeds when we arrived back from anywhere – even if that was just the hot springs. Ava and Eumelia would leave the care of the stallions to the boys, preferring instead to braid Raisa's mane and tail, holding their masterpieces in place with lengths of material. For the most part, Raisa tolerated their attentions, and no doubt if Calla was still alive, the girls would have done the same to her.

My father and Nasrin arrived at the stables, along with Archippos and the other children. Father took one look at Skotos and burst out laughing.

"Do not be so hasty to laugh, Father," I warned, pointing to Skaris' pen.

"Skaris?" he gasped, his mouth hanging open when his eyes found his horse.

Nasrin joined him outside the pen, her own grin forming as she looked him over. "If I did not know better, I would think Skaris was with foal," she laughed, laying her hand on my father's arm.

Father shook his head, ducking beneath the wood panel and reaching out to stroke the white and tan of Skaris' nose. "You have been well cared for indeed, my old friend," he said, accepting the nuzzling from Skaris.

"Have you come to take him away again?" the small child beside him asked, pausing mid-stroke.

"We have. We must return to our home," Father replied, his tone gentle.

"Oh," she murmured, removing the brush from Skaris' coarse hair and sliding her fingers across the implement, her eyes following their progress.

"You are fond of Skaris?" Father asked.

"Very much. Though he is large, he is gentle and has allowed me to ride him almost every day."

"We have all ridden him. He never throws us off or rides too fast," the eldest boy added.

"And you would be very sad if I took him away again?"

"Oh yes. He is the most wonderful horse I have ever known. He is my best friend."

"I see," Father nodded. He considered the small figure before him and I hid a grin. Archippos' daughter possessed the same look Ava often had when it came to her grandfather; he hated to see her upset and gave into almost any request she made of him.

Father lowered himself onto one knee, his finger lifting the small chin so the girl met his eyes. "Perhaps it is time Skaris was allowed to enjoy his old age. He has been a faithful companion for many winters but his body is not as able to keep up with his want to join me any longer. Would you be happy if he remained here with you?"

"Oh yes, please," the girl cried.

"But Father ... are you certain?" I asked quietly, wondering how he could decide so easily to leave his faithful companion behind.

"I am. Skaris has served me well and deserves to see out his days being pampered and waited on by those who can best do so. I am getting too old to journey about. I always intended to make this trip my last," he replied.

"Trachis is our home now, it is where we wish to find ourselves for the rest of our days," Nasrin agreed, slipping her arm through my father's and helping him to his feet. "Raisa is strong enough to carry both of us home."

Father spoke quietly into his horse's ear, receiving a number of audible breaths and foot stamps in return. "Skaris is agreeable to remaining here with you," he told the children.

They cheered, crowding around Skaris and my father and hugging them both.

After a moment Archippos called to his children and gripped my father's arm to signal their agreement before herding his brood out of the stable again.

"I too shall take my leave. I am eager to clean up before we eat," Nasrin said.

"We shall not be far behind," Father nodded. "I am looking forward to a hot meal and a softer bed than we have had the past few moons," he added when we were alone.

"We are staying overnight? Why do we not press on towards home straight away?" I asked.

"After four moons away, what is another night? Your body shall thank you for the rest tomorrow."

"But …"

"Look, I know you miss them, but I promise it shall not be long until you see your princesses again. Come, eat, rest."

I wanted to argue the point but the offer of a soft bed and a hot meal *was* appealing, as my rumbling stomach attested to. "I shall send a messenger at least. Alexis and Ava deserve to know we are well, and that we shall be back in Trachis in a few days."

Father nodded and draped his arm over my shoulders, steering me out of the stable and towards Archippos' house. "Archippos has a man who can deliver such a message."

"Good. And you are *truly* certain of your decision for Skaris to remain?" I asked, allowing myself to be guided towards the muted lights.

"Yes. I shall no longer join you and the soldiers when you travel – my work shall be solely as a metalworker and celator now. With the amount of time that takes up, I shall not be able to care for Skaris as I always have. It is best he remain here, free to roam, whereas I shall remain in one place."

"I miss the travelling sometimes," I admitted after a moment. "Though the soldiers and I are not in Trachis all the time, we do not journey as you and I used to."

"No, and you are fortunate that you can still leave with the army, even though you are a *princess*," he grinned.

"True," I nodded.

"This is the right decision for me. Now come, we shall enjoy Archippos' hospitality and greet the dawn from the warmth of his comfortable home." He squeezed me briefly before allowing his hand to fall from my shoulders and grip the wooden door.

"I shall find Archippos' man before I join you," I said, standing aside to allow him in.

He held my gaze for a long moment before finally nodding. "Do not be long. I shall set aside a plate for you."

I returned his nod.

I had tossed and turned from the moment I said goodnight to my father and Nasrin until sometime well before dawn when I could not stand it any longer. I fumbled my way into my tunic and armor and crept about the house, gathering food, refilling my waterskin and adding apples to my bag for Skotos. When I stepped outside, the moon was still high and surrounded by clear darkness and twinkling lights.

Though I had made little noise, my father was leaning against the stable doors by the time I got there. "At this rate your poor messenger boy shall not arrive before you," he noted with a quiet laugh.

I could not hide my own grin, shrugging as he opened the door for me. "I cannot remain. Not when we are so close to home."

"I understand, and I expected nothing less. You recall the route to take you to Trachis?"

I nodded. "I do but I shall follow the inland path rather than the sea as we did on our way here. In Skotos' current condition, he shall not be able to handle that terrain. Having him enter the mountains past Parnassos shall be challenge enough I believe."

"It shall. Do not forget that you cannot drive him as hard or for as long as usual. He shall need regular breaks for rest."

"I understand." As much as I wanted a quick return to Trachis, I knew I would heed my father's words – I did not want my dear friend's heart to give out and cause us to return home less *two* members of our family – which is how I thought of Skotos and Skaris.

"You shall have to do the same with Raisa; she is not used to carrying two people such a distance."

"We shall," Father nodded, opening his arms and pulling me to his chest. "Be safe, Daughter."

"And you," I replied, squeezing him tightly.

"I shall see you again within the moon."

I nodded again, settling my bag at Skotos' rump and attaching it with a long rope. I swung myself onto his back and Father removed the wooden planks so we could leave.

"Please thank Archippos again for the care he gave Skotos," I added as

Father returned the beams to their place.

"I shall." I gave him a last wave and headed out into the clear night, allowing the light from the moon to guide Skotos and me north towards home.

Keeping the tall, dark shadow of the Parnitha Mountains on my left, Skotos and I made good time during the dark of the night, reaching the village of Orchomenos and its lake, Lake Copias just after lunch. I had last been at the lake with Thaddeus when he and I met Cleomenes. It had been a brief meeting with the King of Sparta, but one which saw him agree to a personal alliance with me in order to ensure I was worthy of marrying a princess – even if I was the only one who believed such an alliance was warranted.

As Skotos and I travelled through the wide Cephissus Valley and entered the Oetaea Mountains later in the afternoon, I caught glimpses of the Euboean Gulf far off to the right. As dusk set in, I quickened our pace, knowing Oetaea was the last major mountain range separating me from Alexis and Ava, but stopped a short time later for Skotos' sake. I gathered twigs and tinder and lit a fire, keeping watch while Skotos ate his apples and then slept.

5

Night had long since fallen by the time we arrived at the stables in Trachis the following day. I removed the bag from Skotos' back, ensured he had some food in his pen and gave him the barest of brushes before I left again.

I headed directly to the bathing area, the water heating in the cauldron above the fire just as I had requested, and the messenger boy from Oropus awaiting my arrival. It was not just news of my health and return I had sent with him, but instructions for what I wanted when I arrived. The first had been confirmation my family was well, the second, a hot bath.

"The princess slumbers already and the king and queen have your daughter for the night," he reported as I shut the door.

His labored breathing suggested he had not long arrived himself and had rushed to ensure everything was as I had instructed. Perhaps my father had warned him that I would not be far behind. I grinned inwardly and nodded to the young man.

"I owe you thanks for doing as asked," I said, holding my arm out. "You shall find an empty room across the courtyard beside the walkway at this end. Sleep well this night and gather your strength for your journey home."

"My thanks," he replied, clasping it in return.

I nodded to him again and waited until he had let himself out of the room before shedding my armor and tunic. I bathed quickly, not bothering to wait for the water to heat any more, such was my eagerness to see my princess again. I pulled on a fresh tunic and made my way along the southern side of the palace to the central chamber. I placed my shield, sword and cuirass in Ava's room and stepped across to the one I shared with Alexis.

I attempted to open it but found it locked – Alexis must have the wooden piece in place on the inside. I was glad she did so in my absence. I knocked, waiting impatiently for the reply.

After a number of long moments, Alexis' question came. "Who is it?"

"Your wife," I replied.

"My wife? How can I be certain it is so? Prove you are who you claim to be." I heard the grin behind her words and my own broke out.

I thought for a moment before replying. "The first time I kissed you was in your room, the one across this chamber, which now belongs to our daughter. We had not seen one another for a few days and were on our way to the agora with Hesper."

There was a slight pause before Alexis spoke again. "There are a number of people who know that. What else?"

Still grinning, I lent my head against the wood, lowering my voice slightly. "You told me that you slept naked as the day you were born well before I learnt that truth for myself."

Alexis laughed – a sound I had sorely missed – but did not open the door. "What else?" she asked instead.

I allowed a growl to escape, but answered her again after barely a moment's hesitation. "You have the most beautiful body I have ever seen, including the women who presented themselves to you at Aphrodite's temple when we visited Corinth together."

I had barely finished speaking before the lock was lifted and the door pulled open. Alexis stood, naked, before me. My eyes travelled over the familiar flesh, taking in every contour from bottom to top before I pulled her against me, the heat of her skin meeting mine through my sheer tunic. I kissed her deeply, reveling in the contact and feel of her in my arms again.

"I have missed you," I whispered when we parted.

"And I you. More than you can imagine."

I closed the door with one hand, my other still keeping my lover against me. I kissed her again and took her to our bed. I stretched out against her, our arms and legs entwining almost without conscious thought. Alexis kissed my throat, nuzzling at my collarbone as her fingers worked the metal fibula from the material at my shoulder.

"How is it you smell so good? I expected to see you covered head to foot in dirt or dried blood."

I grinned, sighing as Alexis removed my tunic entirely. "That was probably close to what I looked like before I arrived at our door. I bathed only briefly before coming to you, which I hope you appreciate as I have not enjoyed heated water on my skin since I left."

"I feel privileged you spent so little time in the bathing area … and appreciate it very much."

Alexis repositioned herself atop me, her lips finding mine. Her hands began their own journey, exciting me as much as her flickering tongue. I slid my palm down her back, my hand coming to rest against the small of her back. She sighed against my lips and opened her thighs. I slid one of mine between, my heartbeat doubling on contact as I felt her wetness. Gripping her backside, I guided her against me, her breaths short and fast as I pushed her closer to her end. The pressure and movements against my skin heightened my own senses and when her teeth found my lip, I cried out not only in surprise, but with unabashed desire.

Keeping her pressed hard against me, I rolled so I lay on top of her, moving rhythmically until I felt the first spasms of her release rising to the surface. I followed her into the welcome oblivion of ecstasy I always felt when we came together in such a manner, my movements unceasing until the final waves of our shared love abated. I fell back onto the bed, drawing Alexis with me. We did not speak for a long while, content to simply enjoy one another's embrace after so long apart.

"How is Ava?" I finally asked.

"She is well, though she has missed you."

"I have missed her too."

"I have been worried about her," Alexis murmured.

"Why?"

"She has had nightmares, they began not long after you left."

"About what?" I asked, lifting Alexis' chin so our eyes met.

"She said she did not recall any specifics when she woke."

"You did not believe her?" I asked with a frown.

"Not necessarily. She did not appear to be keeping anything from me, but I allowed her to sleep beside me and …" she paused.

"What?" I asked, concerned now at Alexis' hesitance.

She blew out a deep breath before she replied. "She would speak or cry out before she woke sometimes and I … I thought I heard her say Ares' name. More than once."

"Ares?" I repeated, my concern growing into fear.

"I could have been mistaken," Alexis added quickly, her own frown marring her forehead.

"Have you had dreams of him?" I asked.

"No. Have you?"

"Some, yes. Barely any since I have been gone though."

Alexis propped herself up on her elbow. "Do you believe it to be connected? What do you think it means?"

"I do not know. Perhaps it is just coincidence, or perhaps it was not *Ares* she said at all."

"That is true, as I said, I could have been mistaken. Often I was quite asleep when she woke me; she could have even been saying air," Alexis shrugged. "Besides, with you here, I know we are safe."

"Always," I assured her, leaning over and capturing her lips again. "Do you want to collect Ava from your parents and bring her here? It would be a nice surprise for her to wake and find me in bed beside her."

"Perhaps we could just allow her to discover you on her own in the morning. I want you all to myself for a while longer," she replied, pressing her body the length of mine.

I grinned, kissing her again as my hands found the curve at her hip. "Mmm ... as you wish, Princess."

*

"I have missed this," Alexis yawned, snuggling back into me as I wound an arm around her.

"So have I," I replied, placing a kiss in her hair. "I have not enjoyed falling asleep alone, or waking without you beside me."

A knock at the door halted our conversation, Hesper's voice carrying through the wood to us. "Alexis, are you well? I saw Ava was still with the king and queen this morning."

Alexis untangled her limbs from mine and pulled a himation around her body as she crossed to the door and opened it. "Skylar has returned," she told Hesper.

"Ah, that explains it," her friend replied, poking her head around the door and giving me a wave. "Good morning," she smiled. "It is good to see you again."

"And you."

Hesper disappeared again, dropping her voice as she spoke – I could just imagine what she was saying to my wife, and Alexis' laughter confirmed it.

"Send Ava over, she has been eagerly awaiting Skylar's return as well," Alexis said before closing the door. She returned to the bed, discarding the himation and reaching for her chiton. "Our daughter shall be here momentarily, you should dress," she told me.

I opened the covers and raised an eyebrow as I took her hand. "I could, but ..." Alexis attempted to frown, but could not keep the grin from her lips as she shook her head. I pouted but released her fingers, rolling off the bed and pulling my tunic on. "I am eager to see her again sooner rather than later but I hope you and I are alone again before too long."

"Oh, you can count on that," Alexis promised, pushing up onto her toes to kiss me.

I wrapped an arm around her waist and pulled her close, deepening our kiss and re-firing the heat of our passion deep in my stomach. I broke the contact only when the door to our room opened.

"Mumma!" Ava cried, running towards us. I barely managed to release Alexis before Ava jumped up into my arms.

"Hello, my darling," I replied, holding her tightly as she wrapped her arms around my neck. "Have you grown since I last saw you?"

"I might have," she shrugged. "You have been gone a long time," she added with a frown.

"I have. Too long. I missed you very much."

"But you shall tell me about where you have been and what you have seen?" she asked as I returned her to the ground.

"I shall tell you what I can," I nodded.

Ava took my hand, leading me to the bed so I could begin the tale but before I could, there was another knock at the door. Alexis opened it, revealing the eager faces of Eumelia, Nikomachos and Lysistratos.

"Good morning."

"Welcome back."

"Are you well?" they cried, their gazes finding me and words tumbling over one another excitedly.

"Can Ava join us at the barracks this morning? Kleitos, is going to spar with *real* weapons against Moeris and they have invited us to watch," Nikomachos asked.

Ava looked between her friends and Alexis and I. I saw she was torn between the story I would share with her, and missing the show.

I smiled and picked her up again, hugging her tightly before speaking quietly at her ear. "Go on. I am not going anywhere. I might even come and watch a bit later."

"Promise?" she asked, pulling back from me, head to the side reminiscent of her mother.

"I do." I placed her back on the ground, smiling again as she ran to Eumelia's side and joined the other three in dashing from the room, questioning each other on how they thought Lysistratos' brother would fare against Moeris.

Alexis closed the door behind them, turning to me with a smirk. "Well, now that we are alone again ... and there is no chance of us being interrupted ... what *shall* we do with ourselves?"

"Well actually, I really want to watch the training," I told her, attempting to keep a straight face.

"Do you?" Alexis asked, shedding her chiton and stalking towards me.

I swallowed, my eyes tracing her curves. "Er ... no not really."

"Good choice," she purred, sliding the fibula from my tunic and pushing me back onto the bed. "It shall be far more interesting here," she assured me, covering my mouth with her own so I could not reply.

6

I settled back into life at the palace with my family easily over the next few moons, Agrias helping that by announcing that I did not have to join him and the other delegates at the assembly of the Great Amphictyonic League in Delphi, due to my recent absence in Naxos. His words were met with gratefulness from me, and unsuppressed joy from Alexis and Ava.

I continued to train with the soldiers each morning, my afternoons spent with Ava and the other children at the agora or at the palace, or, if I was fortunate, with Alexis at the hot springs or alone in our room.

With the arrival of the New Moon of Gamelion, a messenger came from Cleomenes, asking me to travel to Sparta and join him in meeting a Satrap of Miletus. I was reluctant to leave home again so soon and had considered taking Alexis and Ava with me, but with a Persian on Greece shores, and my own recent involvement in Persian affairs, I would not put my family in danger if the Satrap knew I had been in Naxos. Instead, I left my family with the promise that my return would be much quicker than when I had travelled to Naxos, and that I would be in far less danger.

7

Later 10th, Moon of Gamelion

The king of Sparta sat proudly atop his steed and waved to the three men hurrying between the small huts at the base of Mount Parnonas. They returned his greeting, though I was not certain they recognized their leader; Cleomenes wore none of his usual armor, or the famed red himation of his people – just a plain tunic with his sword fastened at his side. The only indication he was of the royal house was the ring he wore on the smallest finger of his left hand, and we were too far away for the men to see its distinctive two-sided shape.

"Apologies my request to come to Sparta sees you miss the celebration of your daughter's birthing day. How old is she now?" Cleomenes asked.

"Nine winters," I replied, Skotos trotting along beside the king's horse. "I have never missed the day before, though both Ava and Alexis understand you would not call on me unless it was important."

"Indeed," he nodded.

The Satrap that Cleomenes had asked me to come to Sparta to meet was Aristagoras – the Persian who Megabates had said now owed his kin money following the failed Naxian invasion. Apparently Aristagoras had an urgent request, but so far I had not seen him. My patience with the man was wearing thin; he claimed the voyage had tired him and idled the days away at Cleomenes' home, enjoying the attentions of the slaves and women who fawned over him. I could do naught but wait, as Cleomenes did, for Aristagoras to tell us why he had come to our shores. In the meantime, the king and I rekindled the friendship we had made ten winters ago in Athens, and spoke some of what had occurred since for us both.

"Allow us to turn thoughts from business for this day and have them land instead on something very few in Sparta have ever witnessed, and fewer still approve of," Cleomenes grinned.

Late last night, Cleomenes had asked me to join him before dawn so we could travel half a day south of the city to a small village. It was one he had formed, placing certain people there, though he was vague on the details of what we would find when we arrived.

"You have brought me quite far south," I noted, unable to help returning his infectious smile.

"Yes. This is Rachi," he announced, spreading his arms wide to take in the huts and mountains just off the small path we followed.

There was not much to see, and to call it a village was perhaps generous. Ten or so homes clustered close together in no apparent conformity, dirt separating them by perhaps ten feet or so. We had followed the Eurotas River for most of the way to Rachi, but it did not run nearby at this point.

"Now you are considered a princess of Trachis, do you favor royal purple garments as your family has always had?" Cleomenes asked.

"On some occasions, though mostly I remain in my cuirass and tunic."

He nodded. "Have you ever wondered why purple is only worn by the most important?"

"Because of its cost," I replied. "When I was in Hermione many winters ago, I met a woman who supplied wool from her sheep for the process."

"Indeed. Did you spend time with the dye makers of Hermione?"

"No."

"Why ever not? Your father did not wish you to see how the dye was made?"

I shrugged. "Perhaps he did. We were in Hermione for two moons, but we learnt of other trades – perfume mostly – before we headed north again."

"Well then, I should be honored if you would allow me to show you how it is done."

"That is what you created Rachi for?" I asked, impressed.

Cleomenes nodded again. "I too went to Hermione during my time in Athens; it is one of the reasons I did not join you in Stratos as I intended. I was fortunate enough to make friends with a man who earned much coin from the process he perfected and he taught me what to do."

"Was he not concerned you would establish your own trade and take his customers?"

"Perhaps, though he never spoke explicitly of it. He did not see me as a threat as Spartan law has always prohibited dyers from establishing themselves in the region. It was seen as falsifying nature. But as king, I had

26

the power to overturn the decision and enact a new law, and I did. It was not taken favorably by those of the old thinking, but they could not stop me, and so Rachi was born. We are well established but even so, I have ensured our trade route is not the same as Hermione's as respect to my friend for allowing me his knowledge. *They* produce fine robes entirely of purple with a broad vertical white stripe down the center, so I have ensured our patterns differ from theirs."

"Where do you export to? Where does Hermione?"

"Hermione's products are sent as far east as Tyre in Persia where they are used to clothe their kings."

"Persia?" I murmured, wondering if King Darius himself wore garments made from Greek dye.

"Yes. We rear our own sheep here, though we do not have enough, and we too purchase the materials from the women of Athens. Mainly our finery makes its way to Corinth, where they have become known for the exquisite and exotic colors. We also send the dye itself to other workshops in Greece. Meliboea in Thessaly is quickly establishing itself as a quality dye center, as well as Syracuse and Tarentum in the far west."

Cleomenes paused, his thoughts turning inward and I allowed him his private reverie before he spoke again.

"I know what people say about me. I know they do not understand why I favor my wine unmixed, or why I would be interested in such matters as this. But I find those people to be very short sighted. They are afraid of what they do not understand and are quick to speak ill of those who show interest in them. What they do not realize is that much can be gained by learning of other ways and other peoples."

"Indeed it can," I agreed.

"What I learned in Hermione was fascinating, and the coin it brings in benefits our people and our city; I am able to retain the finest metalworkers for our workshops, which ensures our army has the very best weaponry and armor ... Come, our destination is a little further on."

Cleomenes and I travelled another quarter candlemark before we came to a lone building with solid walls and smoke coming from the middle of its roof. The king dismounted and tied his horse to a low hanging branch as I did the same with Skotos.

"Unlike in Hermione, we have found a way to prolong the life of the creatures needed to produce such dye. It is them I wish to show you," Cleomenes said as we made our way to the small building.

The stench of old fish was especially ripe the closer we got and I wondered exactly what *creatures* he spoke of for his process. The door opened before he could raise his knuckles to rap on the wood and a man around his age stepped outside. They embraced briefly before Cleomenes introduced him to me as Pelagios, and me to him with my official title as

Princess of Thermopylae.

After my marriage to Alexis and the alliance with Cleomenes was made official, Agrias and I decided that Alexis and I would be known as Princesses of Thermopylae, rather than Trachis – it was intended to recognize the entire region we would one day oversee, rather than just our town – and that gave us higher standing among Cleomenes' other allies.

Pelagios' eyebrows rose high on his forehead, and he was about to bow in my direction when I held out my arm, taking his in the more customary forearm grip. "Just call me Skylar," I corrected. He appeared far more at ease after we shook and quickly invited us inside.

It was akin to the metal workshop at Ophelos' house in Trachis with a roaring furnace on one wall, its chimney built up through the ceiling, and long clay pipes with bellows on the end at its base to push more air in. Barrels of water and charcoal were lined up to one side, an anvil standing in the middle of the room, and several long tables placed almost haphazardly around it. Their surfaces were covered with a mixture of ore, tools and weapons.

Unlike back in Trachis, there were three *other* rooms also for the process, though Pelagios showed me only two of them. In the first room, clay vessels including spouted bowls and shallow and deep cooking pots – which Cleomenes explained were used to prepare liquids – were scattered across the top of the tables. There was a furnace in there as well, though I realized it was the same one as in the first room; the wall simply cut away to accommodate its width between the two. The second room was filled entirely with amphorae of dye and neither the king, nor Pelagios, were certain how many they had stored there.

We bypassed the third room, though I noted a fire with a three-legged cauldron heating on top of it, the flames below were low, and barely any steam rose from the top. Pelagios continued out a rear door, where six strange vessels were clumped together twenty feet away. They were cylindrical with two handles, similar to amphorae, but marked with vertical grooves on the outside. At the bottom was a gap and a number of flying insects made their way in and out as I watched.

"What are those?" I asked.

"Do not go too near, or you may find yourself stung," Cleomenes replied with a hand on my arm. "They are bees. Insects from whom we collect honey. You know of it?"

"Of course, my friend Hesper adds it to her bread to sweeten it."

The king grinned and nodded. "Here, we do not collect it for eating, but to preserve the fabrics once they have been dyed. Allow me to show you."

Cleomenes led Pelagios and me back inside to the room we had not entered before. It was three times the size of the others with a number of long lengths of material hung from the walls and roof at one end and more tables and barrels along the others. The fire and cauldron stood in the center, much space given between them and the tables and the thick pile of wool on the floor

Cleomenes immersed his hand into one of the barrels. It was filled with water, and when he withdrew it again, he held a long, spiny object I did not recognize. He handed it to me and I took it carefully, surprised to find the fronds were solid but not sharp when I ran my fingers over them and placed it on my palm. It extended from the tip of my longest finger to well past my wrist and its inside was a display of bright orange.

"That is a murex shell. From them we extract the purple dye you see on the materials here," he said, pointing to the hanging fabric. "We have a harbor at Gytheion on the Laconian Gulf, where our fleet remains when they are not at war, and it is there that Pelagios harvests them. I also have men who travel as far as the port at Thebes and to Boulis on the Corinthian Gulf to collect them."

"Boulis is a day's travel southeast of Anticyra, is it not?" I asked.

"Yes. Do you know of the town?"

"I have never been there, but Anticyra was where I first picked up weapons."

The king nodded and continued. "In Hermione, they use murex shells for a deep red dye and the mollusk porphyra, which gives the purple. It is they who, until recently, always provided our military himatia. Now we are able to make our own. The honey preserves the color in the material for a much longer time, so I invested in the beehives two winters ago."

"I saw a lot of white fragments on the ground outside, they are from these shells? Do you crush them to obtain the dye?" I asked, handing the shell back.

"At first that is how it was done. There is a gland inside which we had to extract, crushing the shell with a sharpened rock to remove it. But it was a laborious process as the shells themselves are very hard, and often the rock broke before we had the gland. But Pelagios discovered another way to get what we require."

Cleomenes returned the murex shell to the water as Pelagios took up the explanation. "It is not the gland itself exactly, which provides the dye, but the gland attached to the sea snail that lives in the shell."

"Sea snail?" I repeated.

"Yes, the extraction process is almost as time consuming as attempting to break the shell, but we can re-use the gland time and again."

"How?"

"I found, quite by accident, that the creature uses its secretion as a defensive and predatory behavior, and that by poking at it, it will spit out the liquid we need."

"It was then, we realized we could use them more than once, giving us an almost endless supply if cared for correctly," Cleomenes continued excitedly. "The shells in the barrels here are empty – their snails dead, not from mistreatment, but old age."

"The one Cleomenes handed you was one of my first, almost eight winters ago. It has served me well and I could not bear to bring myself to discard its shell."

"Pelagios brings all his newest finds back in barrels of the salted waters from where they came from. It aids them in adjusting to their new conditions outside the constant ebb and flow of the sea life. He ensures the same snail is not used to exhaustion, often noting their specific patterns and alternating between them to prolong their lives."

"I have spent much time studying where the different types thrive," Pelagios added. "Some prefer rocky bottoms or course sand at depths of between four and six feet, while others are to be found in muddy habitats almost twenty times deeper than that. I have attempted to duplicate their ideal conditions here, scraping out sections of the nearby mountains or digging deep holes in the ground and filling the hollows with the salt water."

"Pelagios has a number of hidden pools between here and the harbor which he tends."

"With such depths required, how do you catch them again?" I asked.

"With wicker traps on long ropes," Pelagios replied. "I place bait inside and weight them with stones before lowering them into the created spaces. The snails come out to feed, and get themselves trapped in the baskets. I then pull them up, freeing them from the net and extracting the clear dye before placing them back in the water."

"You put the dye directly from the shells into the amphorae?" I asked.

"No. I place the collected liquid in vessels and combine it with salt, as the snails are used to being submerged in. I then leave them to sit outside for three days, at which time, the transparent mucus becomes first yellow and then a red-purple color."

"That explains the fish smell I noticed when we first arrived," I noted.

Pelagios nodded, warming to his story as he continued. "After three days, I place the dye into a cauldron over the fire, adding water and heating it continuously for ten days. I have to watch it carefully, for if it boils, the dye becomes useless and I must start the entire process again."

"How much does it make?" I asked.

"At the start of the ten days it would be equivalent to one hundred amphorae of gland secretion and water. By the end, I have one amphora of dye."

"That is all?" I asked, surprised. "How many winters did it take you to gather all the amphorae in the other room?"

"Quite a number, though the colors we have been able to produce make the arduous processes worth it," Pelagios replied. "Unlike others, our purple intensifies the longer it is exposed to sunlight, making it an attractive, and expensive, luxury for kings and royalty."

"Indeed," Cleomenes nodded. "Would you join Pelagios and me in testing the latest batch from the fire?"

"I would enjoy that," I replied.

8

We neared the fire and Pelagios took a length of wood, the end third of which was a deep purple rather than a grey-brown.

"I told you earlier that after ten days I remove the dye from the fire, though that is only if it is the color I wish for. To test it, I immerse a small piece of wool in the dye for five candlemarks. When I remove it, it is of a dark, almost black hue and I take the dye from the fire. A length of material is then submerged until it is fully imbibed with the dark color. If it shows any sign of red, then the dye is not ready and the liquid shall continue to be heated until it is."

"So, if you want to use the dye for the red himations for the soldiers, I gather you do not heat it for as many days?" I asked.

Pelagios grinned and turned to Cleomenes. "This one is a quick learner, can you not find ones as smart as she to join me here at Rachi?"

"I have attempted to my friend, I have attempted to," the king laughed.

Pelagios stepped closer to the cauldron and dipped the stick in, bringing out a dark, wet clump. His face lit up and, with a hand beneath the wool to catch the dark drips, he crossed to one of the tables, placing the wool on top and smoothing it out between two short lengths of material. "Beautiful," he murmured. "Brilliant. Perfect."

Cleomenes and I remained at the fire, giving the craftsman his space. When finally he had inspected the wool from all angles, he turned back to us, triumphant. "This is possibly our best batch ever. Come and see," he waved us over eagerly, stepping aside so we could enjoy the result.

I joined Cleomenes at the table and looked over the deep purple, which was indeed almost black, nodding and congratulating Pelagios. A noise outside caught my ear and I immediately drew my sword from its sheath.

"Stay here," I ordered. Neither man protested but Cleomenes drew his own weapon and nodded in reply when I met his eyes. His reaction told me visitors here were both uncommon, and unwelcome.

With quick, quiet steps I made my way to the front door. Re-gripping my sword, I took a breath before yanking open the wood – almost stabbing Moeris through the throat.

"Stay your weapon!" he cried, fast enough to duck my attack as he placed himself in front of the woman who accompanied him.

"Moeris," I breathed, lowering my sword instantly and shaking my head. "Perhaps next time you would announce yourself, rather than approaching with stealth." I re-sheathed my weapon as Cleomenes and Pelagios joined us at the doorway.

"Apologies. Our arrival was not intended to cause fear. We spoke along the path, I am surprised our words did not reach you."

I had brought Moeris to Sparta with me as dual commander of our army; if there were decisions to be made about Persia or its Satrap, I wanted his immediate input. The woman with him – Cleomenes' daughter, Gorgo – had instantly taken charge of Moeris when we arrived, fussing over his every need and ensuring he ate well and often. She was nineteen winters old, and whilst not as great a beauty as her mother, she was a pretty enough girl with long, dark hair the same color as her father's. She was quite taken with the older soldier – he too appearing to find enjoyment in her company. I was not surprised to find her with Moeris today given their friendship, and the freedom with which she was given to travel in her father's kingdom.

"What are you doing here? Gorgo, has something happened to your mother?"

"Your queen is quite well, King Cleomenes," Moeris replied with a bow.

"We came to tell you that Aristagoras has finally sated his needs and is ready to speak of why he has come. He awaits your arrival at Demaratus' home," Gorgo added.

"Perhaps I should make him wait until *I* am ready to see *him*," Cleomenes muttered.

"I would not advise it, Father. Though he has taken his time, I believe it prudent we return quickly."

Cleomenes regarded his daughter a long moment before giving a curt nod and turning to me again. "Apologies we cannot remain here any longer at this time. Perhaps you shall favor me with another visit south – with your family of course – and I can teach you properly of our dyeing process."

I inclined my head. "It would give me great pleasure to return with Alexis and Ava."

Cleomenes took Pelagios' arm and thanked the man for his continued work. "Come then, allow us to return to the pressing business which awaits us," he said, offering his arm to Gorgo and leading her and Moeris back to the horses.

I took Pelagios' outstretched arm and gripped it tightly. "Thank you for sharing your work with me. I hope one day soon I can return and see the entire process through."

Pelagios tightened his hand in return and smiled. "I would enjoy that very much. If my king trusts you enough to bring you here, then I know you must be not only clever, but have an inquisitive mind which seeks to find answer in all you come across. It was a privilege to welcome you."

"Thank you," I smiled, somewhat embarrassed by his words. "Tell me, do you have other shells such as the one you showed me from the barrel?"

"Many," he replied, releasing my arm.

"Today is my daughter's birthing day and though we have many rivers near Trachis, none I know of contain shells anything akin to those. She would adore one so magnificent."

"Of course, of course," Pelagios grinned. "I would gladly send you on your way with one, two if that was your desire."

"One shall be enough, thank you," I assured him.

Pelagios crossed to the same barrel Cleomenes had taken the murex from earlier and reached in. He pulled out two, looking them both over with fondness. Choosing the larger, he returned the other to the water.

"Here, this is another of my favorites. It is the one I was able to first draw the dye from without killing the sea snail inside," he said, holding it out as he neared.

"I could not. You must keep your first, just as a celator must retain the very first coin he produces. It is the one item you can look upon and see how much you have improved or recall how proud you were when you made it – or in your case, made the dye from it."

Pelagios shook his head, placing the shell in my hand. "I insist. Your daughter shall take good care of it, I am certain."

I drew a breath, but nodded. "Thank you. I look forward to bringing her with me when I return to see you, and she can thank you herself."

Pelagios waved me on my way and I joined Cleomenes, Moeris and Gorgo, tucking the murex shell carefully into the bag I had brought and tying it to Skotos' reins instead of his rump.

"You have a very unique item there," Cleomenes noted as I pulled myself onto Skotos' back.

"I do," I nodded. "I shall gift it to Ava when I return to Trachis, hopefully it shall soothe any hurt feelings she has for me missing her special day."

*

Candlemarks later, Moeris and Gorgo walked in front of Cleomenes and me, their heads bent slightly together as they led their horses towards Sparta. We had made good time but had pushed the horses hard, Gorgo's on the verge of exhaustion before we slowed.

"Your General appears quite taken with my daughter," Cleomenes noted.

"And she with him," I acknowledged.

"Yes," he nodded. "When I returned home after your betrothal to Alexis, I intended to speak to Gorgo about marrying my brother, Leonidas; I knew by then that you were *never* going to take up my offer to marry him," he added with a grin.

"I am glad you bear me no ill feelings for the decision."

"How could I when Alexis is such a fine match for you? She is smooth where you are sharp, a calming influence on a fiery disposition, if I am not very much mistaken?"

"She has many attributes which I am fond of," I agreed.

"I imagine she does," he laughed, shaking his head. "Anyway, by the time I met with Leonidas, he had already taken a wife."

"You were again denied finding him a match, not that it appears he needed you to," I smiled.

"No, that is true."

"My betrothal was many winters ago, you have not sought to find someone else for Gorgo?"

"I have found no one to be a suitable match for her. Not that it concerns her to remain in my home long past the age others of her gender do. And if I am truthful, I find myself quite reliant on her. Not to wait on me or tend my guests as a common slave or wife does, but rather as a confidant. Her insight and counsel I take above all others. Her agenda is never more than to see me safe and for Sparta to flourish. I am certain you are aware that finding one who displays such loyalty to their king can be difficult."

I inclined my head in acknowledgement. "You would not consider either of your other brothers suitable for her?"

"Cleombrotus and I speak little and when we must I find I care for him no more than he for me. Our father's blood ties us, but that is all."

"And Dorieus?" I prompted, recalling that Cleomenes had spoken of his younger brother travelling across the waters to form colonies for Sparta. "Does he remain away from the city for long periods? With your fondness for your daughter, I imagine his constant time abroad does not appear a fine match for Gorgo, unless he allowed her to remain here with you."

Cleomenes took in a deep breath, blowing it all the way out again before he replied. "Dorieus finds himself in Hades' realm these days."

"I am sorry. I had not heard," I said, placing my hand on the king's arm.

"Few people outside of Sparta have. We were closer than many know. It is true that when our father named me as his successor, Dorieus was furious. But it was not because he believed it was his right as first-born son of the king and his first wife. It was because he believed Sparta would never hold power anywhere but in the Peloponnese, and he wanted to be the one to change that.

"Rumors began that he left Sparta so he did not have to obey me as his king, but I shared his desire to colonize lands far off and without the kingship to hold him, he was free to pursue what I never could. We spoke at length about where he would travel to, what he might see, what it would mean for our great city. Each time he returned, he regaled his adventures to me and I listened, somewhat jealously to it all, wishing just once I could join him."

"Is that why you remained so long in Athens? So you could feel as he did?"

"Perhaps, though it was not a conscious decision to do so. It was while I was there, with you and your father that he died."

"And you remained? Why did you not return to Sparta?"

"Why would I? His body was not being returned to us and his wife and son were near enough to mourn him and see his body one last time."

"Oh." I fell silent for a long moment before I spoke again. "When you told Alexis of Dorieus' adventures when we met you on our way to Peraia Chora, you never mentioned he had passed to the Underworld."

"No. I was still mourning his death, in my own way, and I preferred to think of him still doing what he loved."

"Where was he when he died? Was he involved in a battle or did he become ill or injured and slip away quickly from this life and into the next?" I asked, my thoughts on Tritonos and his sudden death.

"He was far away in the west, in Magna Graecia. He died in battle."

"Had he been there for many winters?"

"No. After I took over our father's throne, he travelled far and wide, looking for the most suitable place for us to colonize. Five winters later, he made his first official voyage and sailed south from Gytheion to the Cinyps River in the north of Africa."

"Where is that?" I asked, having never heard of Africa, or the river he spoke of.

"Southeast of Crete. Africa is another large land beside Egypt."

I nodded. "I know of Egypt – it is where frankincense comes from for perfumes." I kept to myself that Nasrin's birth land of Babylon was also close to both Persia and Egypt.

"That is true," Cleomenes acknowledged. "Dorieus and those who joined him were there for three winters, until the powerful empire of the Carthaginians joined with the local nomadic tribes and drove him out of Africa. He returned to Sparta and spoke with me about another fertile land far to the west. After the disaster that had befallen him in Africa, I could not sanction another journey so soon, and told him if he bided his time, he would be able to go.

"He waited, albeit impatiently, for a winter before our seer – Antichares – told him a story of Heracles' claim to Eryx on the island of Magna Graecia. Dorieus believed the seer spoke a prophecy and, as we are descended from Heracles, convinced himself that he was meant to go west and that the colony he created would be successful. I had already left for Athens by the time they met, but when my brother sent word of his intentions to me, I did not deny him, asking him to take men who could bring back the purple dye I had heard so much about."

"You knew of the dye before you were in Athens?"

"Yes. There were a number of Greek colonies already established in Magna Graecia, the colony at Syracuse the most important. Many men I knew from my childhood had moved to the west, ensuring strong ties remained between our cities. It was the ones who settled at Syracuse who provided the purple dyed himations and chitons to our early kings and royalty."

"I see," I murmured.

"The land in the west is very fertile and olives and grape vines flourish, much as they do here in the Peloponnese. It aided in strong trade practices between the two of us, especially if one required extra supplies for their armies, or if the harvest season was unkind.

"Dorieus and those who agreed to join him on the expedition landed in Syracuse. The men who sought the purple dye remained in the city and Dorieus continued on, attempting to found a new settlement named Heracleia near Eryx, which was almost the farthest west they could go on the island."

"Attempted? So they did not succeed there either?"

"Unfortunately, no. The Carthaginians also hold much power in Magna Graecia and joined with the local people of Segesta, killing Dorieus and all his men, except one. A man by the name of Euryleon survived. He sought Dorieus' wife and son, who had remained in Syracuse until the settlement was established, and spoke of his leader's fate. They in turn sailed back to Sparta with the tragic news, speaking of it with the families of the fallen men and the rest of our family in my absence. I received a messenger in Athens barely a week later."

"I offer my condolences again," I said with a nod.

"Gratitude," he replied. "With the passing of time, I find I cannot so easily fool myself into believing that he is still alive and has simply chosen to stay abroad permanently. But it is easier to admit that he is gone, and I can remember him fondly as he was. I know we shall meet again in the Underworld one day."

"You shall," I agreed.

9

We walked in silence for a candlemark or so, following the path back to Sparta, the ranges of Parnonas towering above us to our right and Taygetos to the left. Cleomenes remained preoccupied with his own thoughts and I did not wish to interrupt, so it was not until Gorgo and Moeris returned to their horses and the pace of our journey increased, that I spoke again.

"Tell me of Demaratus. He is co-regent with you, descending from the Eurypontid family whereas you hail from the Agiad dynasty, is he not?" I asked, jumping up onto Skotos' back.

Cleomenes shook his head, as though to dismiss his silent thoughts, and got onto his own steed's back as he replied. "He is. Sparta has had two kings for as long as anyone can recall; the reasoning being that a single king could wield too much influence over his people and become corrupt. This way, one man can ensure the other does not become so."

"You come together to decide all matters of the state?"

"For the most part yes, our primary functions are religious, judicial and military matters. We maintain communication with the sanctuary at Delphi, which as you are aware, is very influential in our politics."

I nodded in acknowledgement. "Do you and Demaratus see eye to eye?"

"Ha! Not at all. Demaratus has been co-regent for five winters less than me, having succeeded his father, Ariston. Almost from the beginning, he sought to work against me. You did not meet him in Athens as he arrived a number of moons after Hippias was expelled. He was intent on ensuring

Cleisthenes remained archon and I learned much I did not previously know about my time there and how he and Cleisthenes orchestrated my involvement in the matter."

"Oh?" I frowned.

"Demaratus had long known Cleisthenes, though how exactly they met and where, I am not certain. When you and I first met in Athens, we spoke of Hippias and his tyrannical rule. You know of his brother's death and how afterwards he ruled with a cruel hand already." I nodded, remaining silent as Cleomenes continued. "As Hippias' treatment of his people deteriorated, it caused much unrest and Hippias was afraid he would be overthrown. To ensure it did not happen, he married off his eldest daughter to Aentides of Lampsacus. With that alliance, Hippias secured Persian assistance should he require it."

"Perhaps that is how he was able to insert himself so easily amongst Darius' court after you and I saw him exiled," I mused.

"I have no doubt of it. The betrothal and subsequent alliance became known to Cleisthenes' family even though they were banished from the city. They feared Athens would fall under Persian rule and Cleisthenes, with aid from Demaratus, made arrangements to return to Athens and remove Hippias from rule."

"How?"

"When Cleisthenes' forebears were exiled many winters ago, they aided building the oracle at Delphi. Cleisthenes used his kin's friendship with the priests and bribed them to insist I go to Athens to aid the people depose the tyrant."

"I cannot believe the priests would agree to speak such a lie."

"I would not have believed it either, but I heard the truth of it spoken by Cleisthenes himself."

I shook my head, wondering how, if we could not believe what our oracles told us, we could ever ask them to interpret the answers from our gods in times of trouble. Unlike Alexis and me, most mortals were never fortunate enough to meet a god such as Asclepius or Hera who offered help to them directly – the priests of the temples were our only link to the immortal beings. Without them, would our faith in the gods dwindle until our children's children no longer believed in them? Would the gods themselves abandon us if we no longer prayed to them and told their stories?

"It is a sad day when our oracles do not speak the truth," I said, keeping the rest of my thoughts to myself.

"Indeed," Cleomenes agreed, continuing his explanation. "With Hippias' attention diverted by my arrival, Cleisthenes and his family snuck back into the city, hiding out with friends until they could reveal themselves. Cleisthenes named himself as the new archon mere days after you and your father left. As you know, I supported him, for he appeared an honest man who had grand plans for Athens. He set up a new boule – council – and spoke often of taking Athens to glory."

"Were you not concerned that if he was successful, Athens' strength would rival Sparta's?"

"No. Athens and Sparta differ in so many ways, I had no such concerns then, nor do I now. You may also recall that when we met outside Corinth, I had been asked to return to Athens and meet with Isagoras?" I only nodded in reply. "It was Isagoras who had learned of the oracle's treachery and first told me of it. Cleisthenes had been easily convinced by Demaratus to have the Oracle speak the words to me – given the infamy of our Spartan warriors – and Demaratus believed I would be killed in the city; a Spartan King sticking his sword where it did not belong. Unfortunately for him, I was still alive and well by the time he arrived, and I knew the truth of what they had done. He did not even attempt to deny it.

"I immediately threw my support behind Isagoras, agreeing to stand beside him as he challenged Cleisthenes for rule of Athens. We were able to reveal the truth of Cleisthenes' trickery to the people and once again banished him and his family from the city, successfully placing Isagoras in charge as archon."

"And Demaratus? Did you speak of his involvement in the trickery?"

"I attempted to with the leaders of Sparta but they would not hear ill words against the man. I am afraid our constant battling prior to that time saw them believe I was merely jealous, attempting to cast suspicion where there was none to be found. No one in Sparta, other than a favored slave, even knew Demaratus had gone to Athens; he had kept to his home, citing illness for his absence amongst our people. I could not prove otherwise. For the moment, I allow him to fool the ephors but I have placed men close to him who report his movements to me."

"Isagoras does not still rule Athens, does he? I cannot say I have followed the rulers of Athens particularly closely, but I recall that he did not do so for long."

"No, unfortunately Isagoras was not archon for long at all, a winter at best. He made many errors in his short rule, his greatest undoing his attempt to abolish the boule of Athenian citizens Cleisthenes had appointed to oversee the daily affairs of the city. He also banished hundreds of prominent Athenians from the city."

"Why?"

"He claimed they had stood with Cleisthenes, aiding him in corrupting the Oracle to get into power. He cited that the curse of the Alcmaeonids had reached them as well by their continued support of the family."

"I can understand why he would send them away – he would not have wanted to fall foul of Cleisthenes' supporters now that he was archon, especially if many of them held positions of power close to him."

"Indeed, though he did not have proof of those people's involvement with Cleisthenes, and the council was much favored by the citizens. Many who had supported Isagoras turned against him and he was banished from the city; Cleisthenes and his family were recalled and returned to power."

"Did you also turn from Isagoras?"

"I did not support nor turn against the man, believing it well time I left Athens to its own decisions."

"A wise choice by the sound of it."

"I have always believed so," Cleomenes agreed with a nod.

*

Cleomenes and I hastened our pace and drew alongside Gorgo and Moeris, the princess speaking of the various plants and animals found on the towering limestone ranges of Taygetos and Parnonas either side of us.

"There are few villages between Sparta and Rachi, is Rachi the main settlement between the capital and the harbor at Gytheion?" Moeris asked.

"It is the only inhabited one, yes," Cleomenes nodded. "There are a number of well-known areas close to the city, though our citizens prefer to travel to them during the daylight only, they never remain after dark. Therapne is to the east of Sparta, near where the bridge crosses the Evritos River. It is where I pointed out the shrines when we crossed the bridge," he added, addressing me. "The Menelaion is the shrine dedicated to Menelaus. It stands on the highest mountain within the Taygetos ranges and is known as Profitis Ilias, which is said to have been the king's home. There is another shrine dedicated to Helen in the same place."

"You speak of Menelaus, the King of Sparta, and his wife Helen, who were prominent members in the Trojan War, were they not?" Moeris interrupted.

"Indeed. I am impressed you know of whom I speak," Cleomenes grinned. "Was it Skylar who spoke to you of them?"

Moeris smiled in return. "Though she has shared many stories with us since coming to Trachis, the Trojan War was not one of them. When I was growing up and still called Macedonia home, the tale was a popular one even there."

"And I am certain that whatever you did not know, Skylar offered explanation of – she has always enjoyed learning of past deeds."

"That is true. It is what aids her to be such a leader amongst our number," Moeris nodded.

"What other settlements are nearby?" I asked, embarrassed at the flattering words from the men.

"Xirokambi is to the west, though there is little to see there now,"

Gorgo supplied.

I drew a sharp breath, glad none of my companions noticed I recognized the name. I had not realized we would travel so close to the place of my birth.

"Xirokambi?" Moeris repeated.

"Yes. It is barely half-a-candlemark west from here," Gorgo replied.

"My daughter speaks true. I had intended on taking you there on our return Skylar, though now I am afraid we must hasten our pace to return to Sparta and meet with Demaratus."

"Perhaps there shall be time to visit another day," I replied, though it was a journey I had hoped to make alone if ever I had the opportunity to go there.

"You said there is little to see there *now*. What happened and when did it change from what was there before?" Moeris continued.

"Many winters ago – I doubt Skylar was even born yet – a great fire swept the village, destroying the houses and olive grove alike," the king replied. "There were no survivors, and no one is certain what caused the blaze. Some say it was Zeus' thunderbolts, others say a merchant failing to douse his fire before moving on. The ruins of three or four houses remain but no one has attempted to rebuild them, and no one dares live there. They believe the spirits of those killed still roam through the olive grove, enticing others to join them in the Underworld."

"There are many weapons the gods have at their disposal to cause destruction," Moeris nodded.

"Moeris," I rumbled.

"Fire is but one weapon they favor," he continued, pointedly ignoring me. "We have had our share o–"

"Moeris. Enough," I cut over him.

Kicking my heels into Skotos, I drew in front of my fellow soldier, blocking his path. He pulled on his steed's reigns, halting their progress, as I stared him down. "Excuse us for a moment, Cleomenes, Princess. Moeris and I must share words."

"Of course," the king replied, he and Gorgo continuing on.

Once they were out of earshot, I spoke again, my words low and dangerous. "You agreed *never* to speak of what happened to that army in Trachis."

"And I said nothing specific this day," Moeris shrugged, avoiding my gaze.

"I am certain had I not been here, you would have."

"Cleomenes is your friend. Our friend. Do you believe he would break your alliance if he knew what you had done?"

"That is not why I wish it never to be spoken of."

"*I* believe it would only strengthen his friendship with us," Moeris continued as though I had not spoken. "He would learn we have direct link to the gods themselves."

"A link I wish never existed, as you well know."

"I do, though it cannot be altered. You did not seek it, yet it w–"

"I know what happened in Xirokambi. I know what, or rather who, caused the village's destruction."

"How? Why do you not share it with the king?"

"Because it happened the night I was born. The night my mother was killed and my father took me and hid me away from my mother's kin."

"Oh," Moeris murmured.

I waited a moment before speaking again. "Why is it you feel the need to bring up Ares and the amulet after all these winters? Why would you have told Cleomenes and Gorgo of my link to him?"

"I am not the only one who has had thoughts about the God of War recently, am I?" he challenged.

"What are you talking about?"

"Has he visited you?"

"No."

"But you have felt him nearby; you and he have spoken somehow, have you not?"

I exhaled loudly before replying. "How did you know?"

"On our journey here you called out his name in your sleep."

"Speak of it with no one. I mean it, Moeris. They are only dreams."

"Are they? You are concerned for what they mean, for how frequent they are, is that not true?"

"I do not know what they mean. I can only hope that my father and Alexis can keep Ava safe if they need to before I return."

"So why not speak of it with Cleomenes? Perhaps he shall return with us, lend the might of his Spartans to our defenses?"

"No. I shall not place him amidst a fight which would only see his death. For all he has given me, I would not ask it of him."

"I believe that is a mistake."

"It is not your decision. Do not stand opposed to me, or work against me in secret in this matter," I growled. "And do not continue to speak of the gods' powers."

He opened his mouth to question me again, but closed it without speaking, inclining his head in submission instead. I turned my horse back to the path and allowed him to move ahead, following closely behind.

"Is the olive grove still in use? Did the trees re-grow after the fire?" Moeris asked when we caught back up to Cleomenes and Gorgo.

The king regarded us only a moment before replying. "They did, and yes, the olives are still harvested by helots from Sparta, though they do not dare remain there after dark either."

"Helots?" I repeated, not particularly happy that we were still speaking of Xirokambi, but glad it was in a more general manner.

"Apologies, you would not be familiar with the class system in our city. There are the Spartiates, the Helots and the Perioeci."

"I know of the Spartiates; they are the professional soldiers of Sparta," I said.

"I am not surprised you know of *them*," Cleomenes grinned. "Only a full citizen of Sparta can be a Spartiate, and at seven winters old they are sent to the agoge to train. At twenty, they are acknowledged as Spartiates and expected to marry, though they remain in the barracks until the age of thirty. If at that time, the gods have smiled upon them and they find themselves still in this world, they leave active service and go live with their wives, fathering the next generation of mighty Spartan soldiers."

"They remain in reserve until their sixtieth winter, do they not?" I asked.

"Indeed. If we find ourselves in need of soldiers, every man who has trained at the agoge returns to swell our numbers and defeat our enemies."

"That is a different life to those of our own soldiers," Moeris noted. "The men are given the choice to remain at the barracks or in their homes with their wives and children if they have them."

"We have boys and men of all ages who have joined our ranks at different times in their lives. Most are not career soldiers such as you have here," I added.

"We are very strict on our boys and what we expect of them," Cleomenes nodded. "They are taught that loyalty to the state comes before all else – including family."

"I imagine that is how you have produced the strength of the army you are so well-known for," Moeris noted. "And who are these *Helots* who tend the olive trees in Xirokambi?"

"The Helots are our slaves. They carry out the manual labor required by those in our city. They are a people long ago conquered by the Spartans and shall be in our debt for many winters to come."

"And the Perioeci? Are they citizens or slaves?" I asked.

"Neither," Gorgo replied. "They are our tradesmen. They craft our weapons and create the beautiful pottery and cloth we send across the seas and lands."

"They are very beautiful indeed," Moeris agreed, smiling almost shyly at the princess.

"Thank you," she replied, just as demurely, and I hid my own grin at their exchange.

10

Candlemarks later, as we passed the shrine of Menelaus at Therapne, the sun made its final descent behind the Taygetos Mountains. Cleomenes handed out torches and we dismounted from our horses to ensure the flames did not singe their manes or flesh. Soon after, we crossed the wooden bridge over the Evritos River, setting us on the same side of the water as Sparta.

As we entered the city, I was struck again by how different it was set out to how I had always imagined it would be. There were no grand temples; Cleomenes did not live in a palace, even though he was king. The whole place resembled a group of villages simply set up side by side with no real thought as to how the layout should be.

We stabled our horses and walked the short distance to Demaratus' house, the co-regent greeting Cleomenes with a deep frown.

"You have kept our guest waiting. Our food shall be cold … and you bring uninvited guests with you. Is this what caused your lengthy return? Did you seek them before coming to me?"

"Skylar is Princess of Thermopylae, and an old friend. Moeris is head of their army. The two have been visiting with me for many days. Perhaps if Aristagoras had not kept *us* waiting for so long, I would have remained at home to hear what he had to say. Instead, I showed my friends some of the more unique aspects to our town and surrounding lands."

"I am pleased to meet you, King Demaratus," I said, holding my arm out for him to take. "I have heard much of you."

"I can only imagine," Demaratus grumbled, ignoring my greeting. "Cleomenes, you may send the women away, what we discuss with Aristagoras is not for female ears."

"As we have oft-discussed, Demaratus; Gorgo shall remain at my side during discussions with foreigners, and in this matter, so shall Skylar."

Demaratus' jaw tightened and he sniffed loudly, turning on his heel in silence and leading us to the andron.

"No love lost between the kings," Moeris murmured as we followed Demaratus inside.

"None at all," I agreed, returning my arm to my side.

"Apologies for Demaratus," Cleomenes whispered.

"Do not worry about it," I replied, studying Demaratus as we walked; he was attractive enough with dark hair, high cheekbones and a strong chin, though the scowl he wore did nothing to highlight any other favorable features he may have.

"Cleomenes has arrived finally," Demaratus announced.

"Wonderful. I am pleased to see you again, King Cleomenes," Aristagoras smiled, rising from his klinai to clasp the king's hands between his own. Aristagoras' dark hair was cropped short, his neat beard and eyebrows in the same shade. "And who are these striking beauties? Entertainers for us? I must say, I am taken with the soldier outfit of the taller one," he added, his eyes falling on Gorgo and me.

"They are not for entertainment," Cleomenes corrected him, holding his arm out for Gorgo to step to his side. "This is my daughter, Gorgo. She attends me in all matters, this day shall be no different." Aristagoras looked the young woman up and down almost hungrily, taking her hand in his and stroking it. Beside me, I felt Moeris tense, but he had the good sense to remain where he was.

When the foreigner's initial attentions with the princess were sated, his gaze shifted to me. "I have heard that King Cleomenes has only one child, so I must ask, who are you to join us in our discussions?"

"Skylar of Thermopylae," I replied, stepping forward and offering my arm.

Aristagoras took it and we squeezed one another's forearms, his eyes remaining on my face rather than travelling down my body. "It is good to meet you," he nodded.

I had seen Aristagoras from a distance when I was in Naxos, I had been defending the wall as the Persian army – led by him and Megabates – approached. I now knew he had not seen me in return; his face showed no sign of recognition and his weak grip on my arm did not betray his greeting.

"This is the head of our army, Moeris," I added, releasing his arm and indicating the man I spoke of.

"Pleased to meet you," Aristagoras nodded, gripping Moeris in the same manner he had me.

"Now we have finished with the introductions, allow us to enjoy the food my wife and daughters have organized for us," Demaratus suggested, crossing to the doorway.

"An excellent idea indeed," Aristagoras agreed.

Demaratus called out and an older woman and young girl appeared in the andron barely a moment later. They kept their eyes averted, placing steaming plates on the table before leaving again.

"This smells delicious. May I be the first to taste it?" Aristagoras asked, sniffing deeply at the largest bowl in the center as the six of us gathered around.

"I would be most honored," Demaratus replied. I stifled a laugh, knowing the infamous Spartan Black Broth when I saw it.

I took a handful of figs and a length of fresh fish, seating myself on a klinai for what I was certain would be a good show. I had had the misfortune of tasting the foul liquid on my first evening in Sparta – Cleomenes having insisted that Moeris and I try the *delicacy*. To my embarrassment, and Cleomenes' roar of laughter, my mouthful had landed clear across the room. Cleomenes held no love for the broth either, but immensely enjoyed the reactions of those who had not been brought up on it.

Aristagoras eagerly drove his hand into the bowl, lifting out a piece of meat. He tossed it between each hand to cool, the dark liquid dripping onto the floor. Cleomenes joined me on the klinai, a grin on his own face, eagerly awaiting Aristagoras' reaction. Aristagoras shoveled it into his mouth.

"One … two …" Cleomenes counted.

Aristagoras barely chewed twice before spitting out his mouthful, gagging as the meat splattered on the floor – a hound appearing out of nowhere to steal the morsel and disappearing out the door again just as quickly.

"By the Gods! What in Tartarus *is* that?" he managed, retching as he reached for his cup and downed what was left in one quick gulp.

Cleomenes guffawed, slapping me on the back as I joined him in open laughter. Demaratus appeared almost insulted by the foreigner's – and mine and the king's – reactions, his brows drawn together and jaw tightening as he spoke.

"This is the most prized of all Spartan dishes. It is pork stew."

"Pork? It is barely cooked and what … what is it cooked in?"

"Blood, vinegar and salt," Demaratus replied, as though it should be obvious.

"Gods, it is terrible. I mean no disrespect to you, King Demaratus, but I cannot believe you would *willingly* eat such a dish." Aristagoras wiped his lips with the back of his arm, downing another cup of wine and shoveling a large slab of cheese into his mouth. "I must say, I have heard tales of the Spartan diet, though I would never have believed them had I not tasted it with my own mouth," he said when he had swallowed the cheese.

"What have you been eating since you arrived, if not our stew?" Demaratus asked. His tone suggested the Black Broth was all the Spartans ever dined on. I knew that not to be true, though there were some who favored it over all else – quite possibly Demaratus himself given his defense of the dish.

"Fruit and fish mainly."

"Well, it is a pity your palate does not extend to favor the fineness of our broth also," Demaratus sniffed.

"Perhaps it is time for speech, rather than nourishment," Cleomenes suggested, having recovered from his fit of laughter.

"Yes, perhaps it is," Demaratus agreed.

Gorgo filled a plate for herself and took a couch to my left, Cleomenes quickly moving to sit beside her before Aristagoras could, as Moeris joined me. Demaratus and Aristagoras brought another klinai over to butt up against Moeris' right before Demaratus dished himself out a bowlful of the stew and sat down.

Aristagoras crossed to a table by the door and retrieved a covered item, unwinding the cloth as he returned to the klinai beside Demaratus and revealing a slab of bronze. I leant forward, noting that the bronze was engraved with a picture. Aristagoras held it up so we could all see.

"This is the known world; all the waters, islands and lands from Greece to Persia in the east, Africa to the south, Macedonia and Thrace in the north and Rome in the west." He pointed to a small island off the coast of Persia. "This is where I call home – Miletus."

"And you are a Satrap of Persia which is similar to our kings here in Greece," I stated.

Aristagoras looked up, his eyebrows high on his forehead. "I am. You know the ways of Persia?"

"Some," I shrugged. "Though I am not terribly fond of your leader, or of what I have heard of how some are treated in your lands."

Aristagoras nodded. "You would not be the only one to hold such opinions. My uncle Histiaeus is leader of Miletus, but has not been there for many moons. I rule in his stead until he returns. It is because of him that I find myself here."

"How so?" Cleomenes asked.

"King Darius and a number of Satraps, including my uncle, who was already leader of Miletus, campaigned against the Scythians. When they returned to Susa, Darius asked my uncle what he wished for in return for such loyal service whilst they were away. Without hesitation, Histiaeus requested to be given control over Myrcinus."

"What was at Myrcinus?" Demaratus asked.

"It is a strategically important area – controlling key roads out of Persia – it is also highly regarded for its sources of silver and wood."

"Items which have many uses," Cleomenes noted with a nod.

"Yes," Aristagoras agreed. "Darius allowed my uncle's request but instead of sending him home to Miletus to oversee the matter, he requested Histaeus remain in Susa as a friend and trusted advisor. My uncle did so, though it was not willingly; the Great King making it clear that there was no choice in the matter. That is how I found myself continued leader of Miletus."

I said nothing, my thoughts turning to Nasrin and the Greek healer Democedes; they too had been prisoners in Darius' palace at Susa. It appeared the *Great King* believed that all who found themselves in his confidence or at his home, were his to control and do with as he pleased, regardless of their own wishes.

"My uncle served Darius just as he wanted, appearing to remain loyal, but when he found himself alone, Histaeus made plans to contact me and have himself returned to Miletus," Aristagoras continued.

"From what I have heard, that would be a dangerous position to put himself in," I commented.

Aristagoras turned to me, a slight frown on his face. "What have you heard of specifically?"

"That is not of any importance today, I only meant that no matter how close of an advisor Histiaeus was, if Darius had learned of his treachery, he would have recalled such an injury for many winters, and taken his revenge at the earliest opportunity," I shrugged. "Any king would react in the same manner."

Aristagoras held my gaze for a moment longer before nodding in acknowledgement. "I believe you speak with truth. The Great King remembers all."

"I am certain he does," I muttered, thinking again of Nasrin and Democedes.

Moeris leaned forward to address Aristagoras. "What plans did your uncle put into place?" he asked.

"He engaged his most trusted slave to aid him; shaving the young man's head and covering it with a message. He hid him away until his hair had grown back, and then sent him to me. The slave told me to relieve him of his hair, and when I did, my uncle's message was revealed."

It was not the first time I had heard of that particular method of secret messaging – Nasrin had told me that she used it to tell Megabates that she had reached safety after she left Persia. She used it again only once, to advise her friend that she had made her home in Trachis and that she had powerful allies.

"What did the message say?" Gorgo asked.

"Uncle Histaeus told me to rise up against Darius, to claim myself sole leader of Miletus and to refuse to answer to the Great King. Histaeus believed that he could convince Darius to send him to Miletus to put down the rebellion, after which he would remain with us, and the king would allow it to have Miletus remain loyal to him."

"And you readily agreed? Why not simply spirit your uncle away from the king? I am certain it has been done before," I said.

"Perhaps it has, though my uncle did not wish to make the king a true enemy."

"So you did as your uncle wanted, even though it could have meant your own death for such an act?" Cleomenes asked, his eyes sliding towards his co-regent. Demaratus did not meet Cleomenes' glance, keeping his gaze firmly on their guest.

"I had had troubles of my own since I took over leadership of Miletus and my uncle's suggestion provided me with an opportunity to change that."

"What did you do?" I asked.

Moeris nudged me hard with his elbow as Cleomenes hid a grin, Demaratus gaping openly at my question as he whispered my name. Aristagoras however, did not appear perturbed by my directness and replied without hesitation.

"I was involved with a failed attempt to take control of Naxos. I borrowed soldiers, coin and ships from Darius' brother, Artaphernes, Satrap of Lydia. I have no proof of it but I believe someone who accompanied me was determined to see me fail and warned the Naxians of our impending arrival."

"Who would want to do that? Certainly it would not be wise to work against a journey that someone in the Great King's family had sanctioned?" I asked.

"It would not, though it is no secret there were those I did not care for on our journey."

"What causes you to believe the Naxians were warned?" Cleomenes asked.

"How else would they have known to hide away their valuables and townsfolk or gather in their crops and stockpile them, ensuring they had enough food for a prolonged siege? Eight thousand men with shields stood, awaiting the arrival of our fleet, their weapons finding Persian flesh before the first order was given to attack."

"Perhaps they saw your ships heading towards them and their crops were already harvested?" Cleomenes reasoned.

"Perhaps. As I said, I have no proof of treachery, though should I find it, that man would be severely punished."

"As it should be," Cleomenes said with a nod.

I knew full well that Aristagoras' suspicions were correct, Megabates and he had had a number of disagreements during the journey, the result being that Megabates sent word to the Naxians warning them that the Persians approached, and to Nasrin, asking for aid from the powerful allies she had told him Trachis had.

"What was the appeal of Naxos?" Demaratus asked, having been silent for quite some time.

"It is the largest of the islands in the Cyclades group. With control of it, I believed the other islands would be loyal towards me if I requested it. Together perhaps we could have freed ourselves from the Persian yoke."

"It is a fertile place? Good for trade, such as Miletus?" Demaratus pressed.

"Not so fertile, though wine, wheat and olive oil are produced with success."

"So you lost your campaign at Naxos, what then?" Cleomenes asked, clearly uninterested in the feasibility of Naxos as an ally.

"After I was defeated, I could not afford to pay Artaphernes back and am deeply indebted to him and his family, which obviously includes the king."

"So why have you come to Sparta?" Gorgo asked, though I believed it was becoming obvious to us all.

"I require assistance against Darius and Artaphernes. With the might and reputation of the Spartan army beside us, the Great King would not dare invade our lands or hold rule over us any longer. We would be free to rule ourselves and toil for ourselves rather than another. Miletus is a Greek power which has been ruled by the Persians for far too long."

"Have you fled your people whilst you seek assistance from us – leaving them to the hands of those you would oppose?" Cleomenes challenged.

"What measures have you put in place to keep them safe while you are gone?" Demaratus added, his tone softer than his co-regent's.

"I have captured the Persian Fleet commanders at Myus and deposed the leaders of the other Ionian states. They all now stand with me and I am their only ruler. I have given my word that when we are successful against the Persians, I shall remove myself from power and allow the Ionians to govern themselves as they wish, whether that be individually or as a common people."

"We have heard many stories of the might of the Persian army, what news of them do you have?" Demaratus asked.

Aristagoras waved away his words. "Do not be concerned with the stories you have heard, the Persians shall be easy to defeat; they fight with their legs and heads wrapped in cloth rather than helmets and armor. When they are defeated, you shall have your pick of the finest of Persian riches –

coin, silver, slaves, whatever you wish for shall be yours."

"How far is it to Persia?" Cleomenes asked.

"From the eastern-most waters of Greece, it is a three moon march to the heart of Persia," Aristagoras replied.

"Three moons? That is quite a distance," Demaratus mused. Both Spartan kings looked to one another, their fingers straying to their chins as they considered Aristagoras' words.

Gorgo leaned close to her father, whispering words the rest of us could not hear. Cleomenes replied just as quietly, their conversation lasting long moments.

"Shall you not share your thoughts with the rest of us?" Aristagoras asked, shifting impatiently in his seat.

"Perhaps we should have a discussion in private," Demaratus suggested.

Cleomenes held up his hand and I caught the last of the princess' quiet words. "You should send this man away, Father. He seeks to tempt you with riches he does not have and shall only corrupt you if you agree to join him," she counselled, and I wondered if Aristagoras had heard her too – he gave no indication of it when I looked his way.

Cleomenes regarded his daughter seriously for a long time. "You are certain of this?" he finally asked.

"I am," she replied.

Cleomenes nodded and straightened, addressing Aristagoras once again. "We shall not be joining you against Darius."

Aristagoras immediately began protesting and pleading in turn. I watched Demaratus with interest; he felt no need to attempt to convince either man of his own opinion.

Moeris leaned close. "You heard what Gorgo said?" he asked.

I nodded, allowing the deep breath I had been holding to escape my lips. "I did."

I was relieved Cleomenes had replied as he did for if he had wished to go, I did not want our army joining him and I knew I would have to tell him of my actions against Aristagoras' cause at Naxos as explanation. It did not matter that we would now be on the same side against the Persian enemy, I would not risk Aristagoras finding out I had been at Naxos, and endanger Nasrin or Megabates.

"King Cleomenes, please do not be so hasty to deny me of your aid. Consider all you shall gain with an alliance such as mine," Aristagoras implored.

"We are allied with many people," Cleomenes replied calmly. "You must see why our assistance is out of the question; we cannot have our troops so far from home, not when there are whispers that the Argives plan to attack us."

"Have you had the truth of it confirmed? With the reputation of the

Spartan army, such rumors would always be flying about, would they not?" Aristagoras countered.

"If there is even a grain of truth to it, we cannot ignore it. Persia is simply too far away for our men to be should we require them here."

"Please, King Cleomenes, though it shall take time to get there and return to your home, I assure you the benefits of joining me shall far outweigh the misgivings you have." Aristagoras continued. "The women of Persia are some of the finest, and the men of Miletus are supremely wealthy and generous. If you sought such attachment, I would be only too happy to recommend a handsome and worthy husband for your beautiful daughter. Indeed I would volunteer myself to take her from your hands if it would aid you in your decision."

Cleomenes raised his eyebrows, a grin touching the corner of his mouth. "Your offer is generous, Aristagoras, but our decision is made. We cannot send our soldiers so far away at this time."

Aristagoras turned to Demaratus. "King Demaratus, can you not share words with your fellow ruler? Make him understand the importance of this journey? You must see how our two lands could benefit from such a victory. Persia is no friend to either of us and if we succeed in overthrowing the Great King, he shall not dare raise arms against us again."

"Darius has never sought to cross to our lands. He is no true threat to us. On this point I must agree with Cleomenes and deny our involvement in your squabble with your king."

Aristagoras opened and closed his mouth a number of times, looking between the two men before settling his gaze on Gorgo. "Princess, would it not please you to join me in Miletus? I can gift you with whatever your heart desires – beautiful jewelry, the finest garments, slaves to answer your every whim. You shall bear many strong sons who shall bring pride to both Miletus and Sparta."

Gorgo shook her head, unmoved by Aristagoras' offers. She dropped her eyes from the Milesian and moved closer to her father. He placed an arm around her shoulders and addressed the man again.

"We thank you for believing so highly in the might of Sparta. Your journey has been long, though unfortunately for you, it has proved fruitless for we cannot return to your homeland with you. I wish you well with your endeavors."

"You are to take the word of a *woman*? A child?" Aristagoras cried, confirming that he too had heard Gorgo's warning to her father. "You do not seek counsel from your soldiers and those who would stand at your side and mine to free my people from Darius? I have never met a king who would so foolishly listen to his own child above that of his most trusted advisors. Perhaps I have been misinformed as to the stature of the Spartan army."

Cleomenes' jaw tightened and I rested my hand on the pommel of my sword. "Careful now, Aristagoras," Cleomenes warned. "You have travelled here with few men of your own. Should we feel your behavior unwarranted, we could silence you and the others and no one would ever know if you had arrived here or simply fled Miletus."

Aristagoras jumped to his feet. "You dare to threaten me?"

Moeris crossed to Gorgo, taking her a few steps out of reach as the Spartan kings and I joined Aristagoras on our feet.

"That is enough now," Demaratus said, placing his hand on Aristagoras' arm.

The man threw it off, backing away from us. "This is a barbaric place where matters are not settled through proper channels and good sense does not prevail. Councils are not consult–"

"And why must they be if their kings are in agreement?" Cleomenes interrupted. "If Demaratus and I were at odds then perhaps we *would* ask them to aid us in making a decision, but there is none here to be reached."

"Perhaps it is time Aristagoras returned to his room. Shall I see him there?" Moeris asked, ensuring his body was between the Persian and the princess.

"I am perfectly capable of returning on my own. I would not wish to run afoul of *you* any more than I would their Spartan soldiers," Aristagoras replied curtly.

"A wise decision to return to your room," Demaratus nodded. "I shall see your needs are met this night and presume you and your men shall depart our city by the time the moon greets us again tomorrow."

"We shall leave even sooner if they have not enjoyed too much of the sweet wine they have taken such a liking to in this place. From this day on, I shall consider you an enemy of Miletus, and I assure you that when I, and the rest of my allies in Ionia, are done with Darius, we shall not forget how you refused to join with us."

"As you wish," Cleomenes shrugged. "Though I can assure *you* that if ever I hear you are on Spartan soil, I shall put you down myself."

Aristagoras held the king's gaze a moment longer before turning sharply on his heel and leaving the andron without further words.

"I shall see Gorgo safely back to her room, if it pleases you, King Cleomenes," Moeris offered.

"Thank you," the king nodded, turning to me. "Would you ensure Aristagoras leaves as he has said; we do not need bloodshed or to further invoke his fury on this particular journey."

"Of course," I nodded.

"It is rare we agree on much, though in this matter I am thankful it was so," Cleomenes told Demaratus as he joined me in the doorway.

The regent inclined his head. "I am as surprised as you, though I agree that it is far too long for our soldiers to be away with the Argos concern."

With a final nod, the four of us left Demaratus to the rest of his evening. Cleomenes, Gorgo and Moeris headed back to the king's house while I followed Aristagoras from a distance deeper into the heart of the Spartan city. He gathered his men from their women and wine and left barely a candlemark later. I wondered if they would return to Persia, or remain in Greece far from their debts and families. Certainly with Cleomenes' answer they could not go home. Not yet anyway.

11

In the early dawn light of the following morning, I sat in one of the large fir trees adjacent to the barracks watching the soldiers train. I could make out their faces reasonably clearly, but knew I would be mostly hidden from them by the long branches covered with flat, needle-like leaves. My dangling feet were the only possible suggestion that I was there, though with the intense concentration of the soldiers, I did not fear I would be seen.

"May I join you?" a voice asked from the bottom of the tree.

I jumped, grabbing the trunk to stop myself from falling. "By the gods, Moeris! Do not do that," I breathed, reaching down to offer my hand.

He laughed, grabbing hold of my outstretched limb and pulling himself up to sit beside me. "What are you doing up here? You do not wish to join them for some sparring?"

"What do you see?" I asked instead, nodding in the direction of the barracks.

"What do you mean?" he frowned, his eyes following mine.

"Tell me what you see with the soldiers."

He was quiet for a moment, his eyes darting over the pairs of men and boys with their shields and swords, the dust puffing up beneath their feet as they shuffled across the dry ground. His eyes travelled along the lines twice before he stopped, riveted. He saw what I had.

"By the gods ..." he murmured. He watched a moment longer before returning his gaze to mine. "Who is he?"

"Leonidas. Prince Leonidas of Sparta. Cleomenes' brother."

"But he look—"

"Akin my father. I know."

"I was going to say he moves as you do; that same self-assured gait as he calls the orders to his men. But yes, his hair is the same light color as Leandros'."

I nodded, watching the prince yell his instructions. His hair was long, held back with a bright red length of cloth, the ends shaggy and in the same exact shade as my father's. The neat beard he wore was the same color and I wondered, if I saw him up close, his eyes would be the same bright blue I had inherited from my father or if they resembled his mother's.

"He lives at the agoge, though he is due to meet with his mother later this morning," I told Moeris.

"You have spoken to him?"

"No, but after I ensured Aristagoras left, I heard Leonidas speaking with another soldier."

We turned our attention back to Leonidas, neither of us speaking for a long while.

"We were so near to Sparta when I was born. After my father fled with me I do not know where we went. Perhaps we were here. Leonidas was born less than a winter after me. Does the timing not fit?" I mused.

"It does. Do you think he knows his father was not the king? Is it a question you would feel comfortable asking him?"

I shrugged. "Perhaps I do not want the answer."

"Do you believe Leandros knows he is his son – if he is of course?"

"There is no doubt in my mind that Leonidas is my kin. My father has to know there is a possibility he has a son, it must be why …" I trailed off.

"What?" Moeris asked.

"Nothing. It just explains a lot about our travelling."

"What specifically?"

"I have to go," I said instead, shooing Moeris out of the way so I could get down.

"Wait," he said, gripping my arm. "Do you want me to come with you to go and meet Leonidas?"

"I am not going to see him. I promised Gorgo I would visit before you and I left today. I want to leave before the sun reaches its highest point."

Moeris nodded, moving aside to allow me to drop the short distance to the ground and landing beside me barely a moment later. "Should I be concerned at the amount of time you have spent with the Princess of Sparta?"

"You have spent more time with her than I have. Much more," I corrected.

"Still …"

"Moeris, Alexis is the only princess – the only woman – I have wanted for nine winters. I hold no affection for Gorgo in the manner you allude to. *You* are the one who has warmed her bed since we arrived. If I did not know better, I would suggest you ask these questions out of jealousy." Moeris colored ever so slightly and I grinned, nudging him with my shoulder. "I am pleased you are fond of her. Do you intend to ask her to return with us?"

"No. She would not leave Cleomenes, or her mother. And I would not ask it of her."

"Are we to lose you to Sparta then?" I frowned.

"No. My home has and always shall be Trachis."

"Are you certain?" I asked, leaning my head to the side as I regarded him.

"You have taken on a number of Alexis' gestures," he grinned.

"And you did not answer my question."

He exhaled a long breath, his smile fading a little. "We have enjoyed one another's company whilst we have been together, that is true. But that is all it shall be. We have both agreed it is best. If one of us was to leave our home we would not be happy, and neither of us want that for the other."

"If you are certain, then I shall not attempt to change your mind."

"I appreciate that. Though I cannot deny it shall be very difficult to leave her." He drew a breath before adding, "Would it bother you if I was to speak to Leonidas? I mean when else shall I have the chance to meet a *prince* who is also a *soldier*?" he grinned.

"Not at all, though I hope you shall not speak to him of what we have just discussed."

"Of course not. It is not my place. I shall leave the discussion for you, should you choose to have it."

"Thank you. If we meet at the north end of the city in two candlemarks does that give you enough time to speak to him before you … make your goodbye to Gorgo?"

"I shall be there," he nodded, clapping me on the shoulder. He headed towards the barracks as I made my way to Cleomenes' house, my thoughts filled with the man – the prince – who was clearly my brother. Another secret my father had kept from me if he knew. And I believed he did – why else would he have been so adamant in rejecting Cleomenes' suggestion of a marriage between Leonidas and me? I had not thought much about his reaction when Cleomenes suggested it in Athens so many winters ago, believing it was only my penchant for women that caused such strong denial. But now, it made more sense.

It was possibly also why we had never entered the city of Sparta. With the kings roaming about the city at their leisure, had father or I met the queen, king, or Leonidas himself, the truth certainly would have been obvious, and what would that have meant for the royal family? As first born, Cleomenes had probably always been in line for the throne, and it was true that Anaxandridas had taken a second wife to ensure an heir ... but was Anassa allowed other lovers? Perhaps Dorieus was not Anaxandridas' son either.

I reached Cleomenes' house, meeting him as he was exiting onto the street.

"Your preparations for returning home are in order?" he asked.

"They are but I did not want to leave without thanking you for your hospitality, and the gift of the shell for Ava from Pelagios."

"Of course, of course. It was my pleasure, but had I known what Aristagoras had come to ask of me, I would not have taken you from your family. You believe I made the correct decision, do you not?"

"I do. You must settle your own battles and leave the eastern Greeks to fight their own. This war does not threaten our existence so there is no need to get ourselves involved." I replied.

"My thoughts exactly," the king grinned. "Well, I thank you again. I wish you a safe journey."

"Thank you," I nodded, gripping arms with Cleomenes in the customary manner. "When Demosthenes and Hektor return, tell them Moeris and I were sorry to miss them, though we understand the reason for their absence. It has been too long since we saw them."

"I shall. Hektor is still determined to return to Trachis when the time is right."

"And we shall be happy to have him." I replied, giving Cleomenes' arm a final squeeze before releasing him. He passed by me before I spoke again. "Tell me, your father's first wife, Anassa, does she live nearby?"

Cleomenes paused, turning back to me as he answered. "Towards the edge of the city, close to the barracks. Why?"

"No reason," I shrugged. "Do you recall when we spoke of Leonidas at Athens, after Hippias was expelled; you said when he was a child his hair was very fair."

"Yes."

"Were there ever rumors that he was not Anaxandridas' son?" I asked carefully.

"None that I heard, though I was too young to have heard such."

"What of the winters since? Were similar words ever spoken?"

"Not to me," Cleomenes said, his frown deepening. "Why do you ask such questions?"

I shrugged. "Leonidas' hair is still the same color. I just wondered if anyone ever spoke of it."

"Not to me ... and I shall have to take your word on the color of his hair for I rarely see him, and when I do, it is from a distance; he is not under my command when we go to war. Besides, beneath the helmets, it is impossible to tell one man from another."

I only nodded. "It was good to see you again, my friend. Hopefully it shall not be as long the next time," I said.

I saw the internal war within the king, but the tight smile I gave him adequately conveyed that I would share no more of my thoughts with him. He finally nodded in return, allowing me to enter his home as he went about his business in his city.

*

A candlemark later, I watched Leonidas leave the barracks, hugging the woman who waited for him nearby and placing a kiss her cheek. They walked arm in arm through the streets towards the agora and I trailed them from a distance, not having the courage to approach and ask them the questions which burned inside.

I wished I was already back in Trachis with my father. It was he I should ask the questions of. It was *he* who should be here seeing his son and the woman he created him with. Had he and the queen had a secret affair when he was here? Is that why he had never returned? Had he feared the wrath of Anaxandridas? I could not imagine him afraid of the man but then I had never met the previous king of Sparta so could not speak as to his nature.

Another conversation floated through my mind – the night of the banquet in Trachis when I had spoken to Alexis of my feelings for her. My father had told me he had borne no children to his tribe of the Bessoi with his bonded, Irina. He had obviously chosen his words carefully for he did not say he had borne *no* other children but me. Did any of the women he had kept company with have children by him? Did I have other siblings in towns or villages we had visited? And if so, did he know of them? Would I one day find myself face to face with another man or woman who resembled me and my father?

I was so lost in my own thoughts that I did not notice Leonidas and Anassa had stopped ahead of me, Leonidas now facing me as they spoke. I attempted to duck out of sight but I was not quick enough and his eyes settled on me. They mirrored mine exactly – in shape and color. His eyebrows flew high on his brow and his mouth fell open.

"Gods," I cursed, backtracking through the streets. If Leonidas truly was my father's son, and as good of a soldier as Cleomenes and Gorgo claimed, I knew he would follow me.

I was not ready to speak to him. Not today. I needed time to arrange my thoughts, my questions. His mother would surely have them once she learnt who I was and I knew I had many for her. But I needed to speak with my father first. I had heard, and believed, another side before his once before and it had nearly driven an unmovable wedge between us. I would not be so foolish again. I would speak with him and then perhaps the two of us would return to Sparta to speak to Leonidas and Anassa.

If I could convince my father to finally enter the city he had always been so careful to avoid.

Hurrying through the agora, I knew my height would be against me, and an armor-clad warrior stooped towards the ground would only raise questions and cause those nearby to stop me unnecessarily. I had to get away from the crowded street. Unfortunately, rather than thinning out the further I went, the patrons became more numerous and I found my path blocked by their stocky frames at the stalls. I veered down a side street, pressing myself against a wooden door, praying it would not suddenly open as I planned my route back to the stables and onto the north end of the city where I had organized to meet Moeris.

I chanced a peek around the doorway, spotting the distinctive figure of the Spartan Prince pushing through the crowd. His gaze was caught by something in front of him and I took the opportunity to step out from my hiding place and head off down the street, hurrying away from the agora, and my half-brother, wondering how long it would be before I saw him again – and got to meet him properly.

12

S kylar, welcome back. Alexis and Ava shall be pleased to see you again," Agrias smiled, embracing me warmly.

"As I am pleased to have returned to them, and all of you, of course," I replied, gripping the smaller man just as tightly.

Moeris and I had been back in Trachis for less than half-a-candlemark, my father and Nasrin having found us at the stables quite by chance and insisting we go straight to the Throne Room to see Agrias and share with them all why the King of Sparta had called us to his city. I would have preferred to see Alexis, and speak to my father alone about Leonidas first, but I settled Skotos in his pen and followed them to Agrias without complaint, knowing there would be time for both afterwards.

"King Cleomenes is well?" Agrias asked, motioning for me to take Melina's throne as he took his.

"He is," I nodded. "The Satrap of Miletus, Aristagoras, arrived in Sparta with a request for aid against the Persians."

"Miletus?" Nasrin murmured.

"Persians?" Father queried at the same moment.

I nodded. "As we already know, after his failed attempt at taking Naxos for himself, Aristagoras finds himself indebted to Darius' brother, Artaphernes. His own uncle is being kept at Darius' palace even though he wishes to return to his home, and so the two of them devised a plan to rebel against their leader and be free to rule themselves."

"Miletus is still a Persian Satrapy?" Agrias asked.

"It is," I confirmed.

"What did Cleomenes say?" Father continued. "Is he going to assist Aristagoras?"

"He said he was not prepared to send any of his men to aid in the campaign."

"How did Aristagoras take that answer?" Agrias asked.

"Not well, he threatened to remember the insult and retaliate against Sparta when they were done with Darius. He did leave without further incident though," I answered.

"Was he going back to Miletus?" Nasrin asked.

"Perhaps. But I believe he shall attempt to convince another powerful city to join him before he leaves. It would not bode well for him to return empty handed when I am certain he has promised those faithful to him with so much," I replied.

"Athens?" Father asked.

"That would be my guess," I nodded. "When they denied the Persians' insistence they take Hippias back after his exile, they made themselves enemies of Persia, so it is possible they would join Aristagoras now to show their strength," I replied.

"If the Athenians did decide to go against Darius, and they managed to win, what would it mean for us?" a new voice entered our conversation – the queen gliding regally across the room. "Welcome home."

"Thank you," I replied, standing and accepting Melina's embrace before offering her the throne I had vacated. "I do not know. I suppose it would depend how depleted the Persians were after the battle. If their losses were too large, I do not believe they would attempt to seek revenge for many winters, in which case we would have time to come together as a united Greek force, ready for when they turned their attention our way."

"Of course, if the Persians *won*, I cannot imagine Darius being particularly pleased that Aristagoras was able to convince the Greeks to stand with him. He may turn his attention to us anyway," my father added.

"Then does it not beg consideration that we go as well?" Nasrin asked. "If neither outcome can save us from Darius' attention, should we not attempt to inflict as much damage against him? At least then when he comes, we can stand tall in the knowledge that we aided in injuring him, rather than simply being branded as enemy because we call Greece home?"

"You are presuming that Athens shall agree to go with Aristagoras, but there is no certainty that they shall do so," I countered with a shrug.

"You were in Miletus before you left with your daughter, were you not?" Melina asked. Nasrin only nodded in reply. "Did you know Aristagoras when you were there?"

"No, his family was installed by the very man I sought to escape. I ensured our paths never crossed, which was easy enough given that

Aristagoras rarely visited the harbor," Nasrin replied before turning to me again. "We should be in Athens, advising them to rally and back Aristagoras. I could speak of how it is in Susa and convince them to change it."

"That is not our place. We hold no allegiance to Athens. And even if Cleomenes had agreed to join Aristagoras, I am still not certain I would have said we would join him."

"Why? You know what Darius is capable of. Have I not spoken of it with you?" Nasrin insisted.

"You have. But we have always agreed that we would do nothing to bring Darius' attention to us – to you. Naxos was a risky enough venture, and I am fortunate Aristagoras did not see me there or I imagine the outcome in Sparta would have been quite different. For him at least."

"You would have killed him," Melina murmured.

"Yes. For Nasrin. And to keep her friend, Megabates, safe. If Aristagoras ever had confirmation that it was Megabates who warned the Naxians, then who knows what else he might learn?" I replied.

"And who he may pass that information to," Father added with a nod.

"Exactly. Nasrin, I understand your wish to exact revenge against the man who wronged you so many winters a–"

"And continues to do so with my sons now in his court," she interrupted.

I inhaled a quick breath, blowing it all the way out again before I replied. "Their attendance there is worrying, I agree, but their exact intentions are not yet known. We must give Megabates time to find out what their plans are – if they indeed have any. In the meanti–"

"Miletus is part of the Ionian League. There are twelve allied cities. We could easily join any of those soldiers without them questioning our heritage or allegiance," Nasrin interrupted again. "We could fight against Darius without obviously giving our support to Aristagoras. Given the man's infamy within the cities that stand with him, we would always know where he was. If he got near to where we were, we would have ample time to hide ourselves so he did not discover us."

"But we were against him in Naxos, so why help him now?" I asked.

"At times we have fought *against* men of Sparta even whilst we were aiding them – Lykaon in Stratos for example," Father said, laying a hand on my shoulder. "This would be no different. We would be standing against a common enemy as opposed to aiding another."

I only grunted in response; I could not dispute the truth of what he said but I would not concede the point so easily.

"If the opportunity presented itself, would it not be advantageous if we could end Aristagoras' life, as well as Darius'?" Moeris asked, finally joining the conversation.

"Of course, but my point is that we should not involve ourselves in the rebellion brewing across the waters. I did not follow Aristagoras after he left Sparta and I do not intend to have our men follow him to the far east in pursuit of a quest which is not our own. We do not find ourselves beneath Darius' sandal, and I want to keep it that way," I said.

"You do not believe we find ourselves on a certain side of the rebellion already?" Moeris asked.

"How so?" I frowned.

"By denying assistance to Aristagoras against Darius, we have effectively placed ourselves on Darius' side, or at the very least, on any side other than Aristagoras'."

"Be that as it may, should a day come when Aristagoras comes back to stand against Cleomenes, then I shall be at my friend's side. But we shall not face Aristagoras or the Persian forces before that. It is my decision as head of the army and I have made it. Understood?" I growled.

"I also lead our men with you, do I not get a say in this?" Moeris frowned.

"No," I replied. "Not this time."

"As you wish," he said, inclining his head, understanding that for the moment he would not win the argument with me, though I was in no doubt he would not leave the subject alone.

I swept my eyes to the king and then my father. Agrias nodded his approval of my decision but Father hesitated, clearly torn between me and Nasrin.

"I do not understand how you can give such an order," Nasrin muttered, shaking her head, her hands wringing and releasing one another at her stomach. "Though I hold no fondness for Aristagoras, if he and others on the islands want to stand against Darius, then I must aid them."

"I have given my answer," I warned, locking eyes with her.

"You hold no command over me. I am no soldier of this town. You may choose not to commit forces to the cause, but I shall go across the water and kill as many Persian soldiers as I meet."

"Understand Nasrin: this is not our battle. We shall find a time for you to seek your revenge," I assured her. "For now it is best for us to simply see how this plays out and how strong, or weak, the Persians truly are."

"Perhaps we can offer a favorable solution," a new voice entered our conversation.

Spinning on my heel to face the newcomer, my sword was out of its sheath before I saw his face. The young man held one hand up to show he was no threat, his own weapon remaining at his side. He wore the armor of a Spartan but his helmet was tucked under his arm and his shield was nowhere in sight.

I lowered my sword again, a grin tugging at my lips. "Hektor," I said, stepping forward and offering my arm. He took it firmly, gripping me in return. "We?" I enquired, lifting an eyebrow.

Cleomenes' General, Demosthenes, stepped into the doorway, ignoring my outstretched greeting and pulling me into a rough hug. Slapping me heartily on the back, he pulled away again, grinning.

"You have not grown smaller these past winters," the older man noted, taking stock of my frame again. "We were sorry to miss you in Sparta."

"Cleomenes said you were gathering information on the Argive movements," I nodded.

"Indeed. Though for now he has all he requires on that front."

"So you came here?" I asked, gesturing they enter further into the room. "We did."

Our conversation paused as re-introductions were made between everyone, Nasrin tense and yet obviously eager to hear their words as she acknowledged their presence.

"Cleomenes told us of Aristagoras' visit, and his subsequent decision not to travel to Persia to assist," Hektor said when the formalities were complete.

"He also said you and Moeris were in Sparta and that you agreed not to go either," Demosthenes added.

"But it would appear that not everyone agrees with your decision," Hektor observed, catching Nasrin's eye. "We would be happy to accompany Nasrin to Persia. Neither of us wish to have Darius, or Aristagoras, knocking on Sparta's door, and if we were fortunate enough to take down either man whilst we were there, then it would be all the more satisfying."

"No. I have given my answer already," I insisted. "Our soldiers shall not travel to Persia."

"Perhaps I too could offer an option," Father ventured. I held his gaze a long moment before nodding curtly for him to continue. When he spoke again, his gaze was on Nasrin but he addressed us all. "What if we sent just a few of our own men with Hektor and Demosthenes? They could send word to us on Aristagoras' movements and how the battle goes. We would then be in a much better position to decide if our presence was required."

"And if it was?" Nasrin pressed.

"Then I would take you," he replied.

"Father," I frowned.

"I am old enough to make such a decision for myself," he replied firmly, his jaw set in a manner familiar to me as he met my gaze. "You can decide what you want for the army."

Moeris leaned closer to me. "Name the soldiers you wish to accompany the Spartans for this journey, and I shall name the ones next time, should it come to that," he suggested.

My frown deepened as I turned to him. "Did I not already give my answer o–?"

"You did, but that was before we had the assistance of two very capable Spartan warriors," he cut over me. "If you wish to keep Nasrin here and safe, as well as your father, this is the right decision."

I growled deep in my throat, though I could see the merit of his suggestion. "Fine." I addressed Hektor again. "I shall name two men, and two men only, to accompany you across the waters."

"We would be more than happy to be those men," Sander said, strolling into the room, Kleitos close behind him. "Thaddeus just informed us of your arrival. It is good to see you again," he added, holding his arm out to Hektor.

"And you as well. It would appear we are no longer children merely playing at soldiers with weapons, but actual soldiers, defending our people and our homes," Hektor noted, looking his old companions over before taking each arm in his own.

"A surprising outcome for our younger selves, no doubt," Kleitos agreed.

"Indeed," the older boy smiled.

I threw up my hands. "Is there a point to me being head of the army? It would appear I hold no power, or the ability to make the decisions I see fit for our town," I grumbled.

I could not be truly upset though, for I knew that the final decision never was truly *just* mine, and I did trust the two young men to adequately carry out any task they were given.

"So you shall allow us to go?" Kleitos asked enthusiastically.

"I shall. But ensure you return as the Spartans do – *with* your shields, not upon them." I replied with a nod.

"As an added precaution, we shall give you shields which do not bear our picture," Father said.

"An excellent suggestion," Demosthenes agreed.

"With the three of us together again, we finally have the opportunity to do something good rather than foolish, do you not agree?" Hektor asked his friends.

"It is about time," Sander agreed with a nod, Kleitos' just as emphatic.

"It is decided then," Agrias announced. "Moeris, take the men and get them settled with food and wine. Tomorrow you can aid them in their preparations to leave for the east."

"Of course," Moeris bowed.

"We shall take our leave also," Father said, taking Nasrin's hand.

"A word before you go?" I requested. He nodded in reply, releasing Nasrin and crossing to the door with me. "We need to talk about my brother – Leonidas," I told him.

The shock on his face told me everything I had suspected. "How did yo–?"

"I saw him in Sparta. I did not speak to him but it is another secret you kept from me, is it not?"

"It … he never bore mention. But now," he paused. "You should go to Alexis and Ava, they shall be pleased to have you home again and I need to ensure Nasrin is well tonight. Tomorrow we shall discuss … him."

"I shall meet you at the barracks at dawn," I nodded. He returned it as Nasrin joined him and I stepped aside so they could leave.

"It is the right decision," Moeris said, and I knew he referred to more than just the decision to send soldiers to Persia.

"So you keep telling me," I muttered, leaving the Throne Room and heading towards the central chamber and the rest of my family.

13

I pushed open the door to Ava's room, the small torch illuminating her in the darkened room. Her breathing was deep and steady, her long, dark hair fanned out behind her as she quietly snored. I grinned and crossed the room, placing a gentle kiss on her brow.

"Mummy?" she murmured.

"Mumma's home," I whispered.

Her eyes fluttered open, widening at the sight of me. "Mumma!" she cried, throwing her arms around my neck.

"Hello," I replied, placing loud kisses against her cheek. "I am sorry I was away so long."

"You missed my birthing day celebration," she frowned.

"I know. But I brought you a present."

"You did?" she asked, sitting up as I sat on the bed beside her.

"Of course. It is very rare, and very beautiful. Just like you," I grinned, tapping her on the nose.

I set my travelling bag on the bed, taking out the bunched up tunic holding the shell Pelagios had given me. I passed it to Ava and she eagerly unwrapped it, her eyes growing even larger as she turned it over and over and peered into the open end.

"Why is it purple inside?" she asked.

"It once belonged to a special snail that produces the purple dye used in our royal clothing. My friend, King Cleomenes, took me to a village where they make the dye and the man working there allowed me to bring back this shell because I was missing your special day by being in Sparta with them."

"I cannot wait to show it to Eumelia. But … how do snails make dye?"

"We shall visit Eumelia together tomorrow and I shall tell you both then. Go back to sleep now."

"Must I?"

"Yes," I grinned.

With reluctance, she slid back under the covers, the shell held tightly in her hand. I kissed her forehead once more and extinguished the torch beside her bed.

"Goodnight, my darling."

"Goodnight, Mumma," she replied.

Closing the door behind me, I made my way across the central chamber, certain that my return would be just as eagerly greeted by the woman in the room before me as it had been by my daughter, though it held the promise of far more physical pursuits, or at least I hoped so.

I pushed open the door to our room with a grin; if our door was unlocked then someone must have told Alexis we were back, and though her familiar outline showed her curled up in our bed, I doubted she was asleep. I slipped off my sandals and padded across to the side of the bed, the soft mattress dipping beneath me as I sat down. I tucked a length of Alexis' hair behind her ear and leant down to kiss her cheek.

"You smell of Skotos and sweat," she grinned, opening one eye.

"And you smell of roses and home," I murmured, drawing my finger along her jaw and pressing my lips to hers when she offered them. "Perhaps I could interest you in a bath?"

"Tempting, but the water would take too long to heat and I am eager to have you in bed beside me. I do not sleep so well when you are not here."

"Neither do I," I agreed.

"What if I collected two amphorae from the kitchen instead?"

"Sounds perfect," I replied, nuzzling at her neck.

Alexis sighed, tangling her hand in my hair as I drew in the scent of her, unwilling to allow her to leave to fetch the water just yet. "How was Cleomenes?" she asked after a long moment.

I straightened again, offering her my hand and pulling her to her feet. "He was well. Shall I tell you of our meeting while I bathe?"

"I would enjoy that."

"Me too," I murmured, my eyes tracing the soft lines of her naked body as she stretched and reached for her chiton. "Do not be long," I added, smiling again at the sudden pink in her cheeks.

"I have missed you looking at me," she admitted, dressing before she pushed up onto her toes to kiss me again.

"Not as much as I have missed looking," I countered, sliding an arm around her waist.

"Always so competitive," she laughed, pushing me away gently and slipping through the door.

I chuckled in reply and allowed her to leave. There would be time to enjoy one another soon enough and I had to agree; I did not smell particularly inviting at the moment.

By the time Alexis returned, my armor and weapons had been set aside and my tunic was unpinned, but still around my body. I did not believe anyone would be accompanying Alexis back to our room, but on the off chance they were, I remained clothed.

Alexis shut the door behind her and I allowed my tunic to fall to the floor as I crossed and took an amphora from her. She laughed and shook her head, remaining where she was to watch me pour the warm water into the basin on the small table nearby.

"Now there is a sight I have missed," she breathed as I held my hand out for the second amphora.

I smiled in return and set the container on the table. Alexis joined me, immersing a cloth in the water and drawing it over my face. I placed my hands at her hips, closing my eyes and enjoying her ministrations. It truly was good to be home again with her.

"So, why did Cleomenes need you in Sparta?" she asked, returning the cloth to the water once again before drawing it over my chest and stomach.

"A Persian Satrap wanted his help against Darius. Cleomenes decided against it, which I am extremely relieved about. I did not want to have to refuse to join the Spartan army in marching there, or speak with my friend of my involvement at Naxos."

"Do you believe he would have insisted our army join his because of our alliance if he had decided to go?"

"Perhaps. The Satrap – Aristagoras – said it was a three moon march to the heart of Persia. It was one reason why Cleomenes decided not to go; he did not want to be so long from home."

"I am glad. Your time away in Naxos was long enough."

"I know," I murmured. "That is another reason I am glad he did not want to go up against the Persians.

Alexis wrung out the cloth and started on my legs. I watched the long strokes she made which both soothed my tired limbs and started a familiar burning deep in my stomach.

"I saw Cleomenes' brother, Leonidas, when I was there too," I began, enjoying the building heat in my blood.

"He is the one Cleomenes wanted to betroth you with, was it not?"

I grinned. "It was."

"Did you speak to him?"

"No. I saw him but … I now understand why my father denied

Cleomenes so quickly, and so adamantly, when he suggested our joining."

"Oh?"

"He is my half-brother."

"What?" Alexis asked, her hand pausing at the top of my thigh and her eyes darting to mine.

I nodded. "His hair is as light as father's and his eyes are the same deep blue as ours. There is no question of it."

"Have you asked Leandros about him?"

"We are to speak of it in the morning, but he did not deny it when I asked it of him. You would be proud of me – I learnt from last time and did not engage Leonidas before I had the chance to speak to Father about him."

"I am very impressed," she smiled.

"I can only imagine how surprised Leonidas would have been to meet me as well. Perhaps one day soon we shall all go to Sparta and meet him," I said, gliding my hands through her hair.

"If your father does not mind, then we should."

I nodded and changed the subject slightly. "When Moeris and I spoke of Aristagoras and fighting the Persians, Nasrin insisted we join them. I told her we would not be going, but Demosthenes and Hektor arrived and suggested they go, along with Sander and Kleitos and report back on the battle."

"Hektor?" Alexis frowned. "The one who stabbed Grandfather all those winters ago?"

"Yes," I nodded. "He accounts himself well now and your father agreed they could travel to the east and send word for us to make further decision.

Alexis fell silent and I allowed the silence to stretch out between us. Her voice was quiet when she spoke again, having started cleaning my other leg. "The night Grandfather was injured was the first time I saw your hands used to heal someone rather than hurt or soothe."

"I recall how angry you were with me," I said, my hands stilling against her head.

She wiped the last of the dust from my toes and straightened, throwing the cloth into the basin and sliding her arms around my waist with a grin.

"Mmm ... Much better," she whispered, breathing deeply as she kissed my collarbone. "As you tended Ophelos, my anger with you waned. When you returned me to my room, I shut you out because I did not trust myself with you. I wanted to remain angry with you for what you had done, but there was also part of me that wanted to ask you to come inside."

"It was difficult being so close to you and having you so upset with me," I murmured, brushing my lips across hers.

"Those days were not ones I would ever wish to repeat."

"You shall not have to. Neither of us shall." I slid the pin from her chiton and helped it find the floor.

She pressed her body the length of mine. "Thank the gods you came to find me at the hot springs before I left."

"Indeed," I nodded, drawing her against me and leading her to the bed.

Alexis lowered herself onto my lap, her thighs either side of mine. I opened my mouth to speak again, but she shook her head and covered my lips with her own, her hands straying to my neck to pull me closer as she deepened our kiss. I allowed her to take what she needed from me, my hands making a journey of their own across her back and hips as her tongue slipped inside to mingle with mine.

When she paused for breath long moments later, I caught her eye, smirking as I noted that her focus was not on my time in Sparta or the revelation that I had a brother.

"You do not hound me for answers this night. Do you not care for my tales?"

"Always. But there is something I wish for far more at the moment."

I grinned again, tightening my grip on her body and drawing her even closer. "Then ask it of me, Princess."

"Love me," she whispered, kissing me again. Her actions were not as fevered, her hands not so tight in my hair. I understood what she needed and I did not hurry or draw her any closer.

She allowed me to set the pace of our coupling, my hands sliding over her skin in long strokes, inflaming her desire as well as expressing the deep love I had for her. Her breathing changed as I skittered my fingers across the tops of her thighs and over her stomach, but still I waited.

For all the passion and lust we still had for one another, for all the times we could not wait to ride the crests of ecstasy, there was something immensely special at slowing our pace. The anticipation of the next gentle caress. Wondering where Alexis' fingers would touch me, of where I would touch her. The building heat snaking through my veins, warming me from head to toe. The warmth of Alexis' skin mirroring mine. Stoking the flames inside her heightened my own desire and it took all my self-control to remain unhurried. Alexis arched her back, the heat and wetness gathered between her thighs brushing my sensitized body. I growled deep in my throat, my teeth capturing her lip as she laughed delightedly.

"Love me," she urged, her mouth finding my ear when I released her.

She found my hand and placed it between her legs, sliding across my fingers. I sucked in a breath as her eyes fluttered shut. I watched her move above me, eyes closed, pink cheeks endearing, mouth slightly open, murmurs of appreciation escaping. I pushed her to the point of desire, reveling in the sounds and sights before me, her eyes finding mine again as she fell over the glorious edge and her body sagged against mine in the aftermath.

"Gods how I have missed you," she murmured against my lips.

"And I you," I replied.

14

"Skylar," Father nodded as I entered the barracks.

"Morning," I replied.

"Allow us to walk down to the Melas River as we speak," he said, adjusting his sword at his thigh.

"As you wish."

Moeris and a number of soldiers trained in the dusty yard, my father and I greeting each as we passed and continuing out onto the grassed area between the palace and the river.

"I am not certain exactly where to begin," he admitted, his fingertips rubbing at his chin.

I swallowed. I had been the one to broach the subject first last night, so perhaps it would be best for me to begin it again this morning.

"Leonidas does not appear much different in age to me. A winter younger perhaps? I can only imagine that means that we spent time in Sparta after I was born."

"Yes," Father replied, blowing out a long breath as he adjusted his weapon again. "There is less than a winter that separates the two of you. I have considered telling you about Leonidas before. After Ava was born and I went away for a short time, I ... I went to Sparta. I wanted to know if he truly was my son. It was his hair that first made it clear, and when he trained I saw so many similar moves to ones you have made over the winters."

"Did you speak to him?"

"No. I could not bring myself to do so. I did not know if it would cause issues within the Spartan royal family, and with Trachis' alliance with them, I did not want to take the chance of it being broken."

"When Cleomenes passes into the Underworld, is Leonidas guaranteed his place on the throne?" I asked.

"I do not know, but I cannot jeopardize his chance if his people see fit to place him as their ruler."

From what I had heard while at Sparta, Leonidas was certainly famed for his fighting ability, and there were no questions as to his sanity, not as there were when people spoke of Cleomenes.

"The only other time I came close to telling you about him was when Dianthe and Ares came to Trachis. But, at the time, there was so much other new information to learn that I did not feel you were ready to hear all I had to tell you. You were under Ares' influence and your pain at the betrayal you accused me of about who, and what, your mother truly was ran deep."

"I remember," I murmured.

"Afterwards there was so much else to speak of, that we never have. Now appears as good of a time to tell you not only of the night your mother died, but of the days and moons which followed."

"I am ready to hear it now," I replied. "I *want* to hear it now," I amended.

Father nodded, drawing in another deep breath. "As I told you all those winters ago, your mother and I fled from Thrace to Konitsa then travelled south into the Peloponnese region, arriving in Xirokambi where we remained until the night you were born." Pain crossed his features for the briefest of moments but he swallowed loudly and leant against one of the large trees. "I hold much guilt and sadness – even now – that I could not save her that night. But I had to think of you, and I would not take back what I had promised her; to keep you safe. You were barely half-a-candlemark old when the Keres arrived at the house. Your mother sent me away with you wrapped in a small blanket and the barest of supplies.

"They found her inside soon after, dragging her and the man who owned the house outside. Zita killed him as I told you, ensuring I had time to flee with you, but I remained in the olive grove, watching as the pack dove on her gleefully, biting and tearing into her flesh. She screamed and kicked and tore at her attackers' skins until the blood and life drained from her body.

"I wanted to cry out, to stop them, to plead with them to spare her, to take me instead, but with you in my arms, I kept silent. I knew you needed me more than ever. I had to leave. I turned and fled through the small grove, my path lit by a pale moon in front and the flickering flames from the burning house behind. I burst from the trees, finding the way blocked by a rock wall. I gazed up at the peaks of Mount Taygetos that loomed large over the village of Xirokambi and turned north, following the scant path.

"Zita had told me to keep constantly on the move, just as we had since leaving Thrace. She said I must never stay in one place for too long or her family would find us. I ran as fast as I could, not stopping until I was far from the small house and the haunting visions. I sent words of thanks to the gods that you slept peacefully in my arms, knowing none of it. I travelled through the night, reaching Sparta early the next morning. The moon had showed me the way as you slumbered, tucked safe and warm against my body. Finally I stopped, exhausted, beneath a willow tree outside a large temple to Artemis.

"I went inside to thank the goddess for your arrival and offer her bread and cheese from my bag as payment. I placed them on the altar beside other fresh fruit and meat, the smell of which made my stomach growl. You woke, yawning widely and I knew I had to find some honey-sweetened wine for you sooner rather than later. You had barely fed at your mother's breast before her family had arrived and I did not wish – nor could I afford – a wet-nurse to accompany us in our journey; wherever that led." Father's eyes took on a glazed look and I knew he was not seeing me, the river, or the mountain around us as he re-lived that time.

"Do you intend to sacrifice the child to the great goddess, Artemis?" a voice asked. Leandros turned to find a man and woman dressed in fine clothing standing beside a large statue of Artemis.

"Of course not. I have only cheese and bread to offer the goddess and I pray that she knows of my circumstance and accepts my meagre tokens."

"The goddess knows many things," the woman acknowledged, emerging into the shaft of light from the doorway.

She was beautiful. Her dark hair held high on her head by a clip adorned with gems that caught the light as she neared. Her chiton was long, reaching almost to the floor, her sandaled feet peeking out beneath the billowing material. Brass clips held the cloth together at her shoulders and on each arm a bronze bracelet circled her wrist.

The man followed at a slower pace, his chiton also white and finishing around mid-calf. He wore a dark chlamys about his shoulders and a ring of gold around the smallest finger on his left hand. The symbol on the ring was similar to the three-sided shape on Skylar's tiny shoulder, but missing the third line at the bottom.

Skylar began to fret and Leandros turned his attention to her, soothing the child with soft words.

"She appears to be hungry," the woman said, approaching and stroking Skylar's forehead.

"Yes, I shall buy honey-sweetened wine for her in Sparta," Leandros replied.

"She cannot be more than a few days old. She needs her mother to suckle from. The woman does not travel with you?"

Leandros paused, a stab of pain gripping his chest as his mind brought up Zita's face. He shook his head.

"Did you steal the child from her?"

"No. This is our daughter, but my Zita … she was … killed last night, less than a candlemark after Skylar was born," Leandros replied, hugging Skylar to his chest.

"I mourn for your loss," the woman murmured placing a hand on his arm. "Do you intend to keep her and raise her yourself?"

"Of course, she is my kin and I shall always be with her, protecting her from harm."

"We have much wine and honey at our home, would you join us and allow us to tend to your needs, and the needs of your daughter?"

"I would be grateful for such an invitation, I have walked all night to find safety for the two of us," Leandros replied, putting his finger between his daughter's gums. She gripped strongly and closed her eyes again.

"Perhaps you shall grant us a gift in return for our hospitality," the man said, speaking for the first time.

"Of course, name your wish and I shall provide it willingly. I have many skills and have spent much time in physical pursuits as well as on finer work with my hands."

The man and woman exchanged a look before the man nodded slightly. "Your height and fair-hair marks you as a northerner, and though you speak Greek fluently, I detect a hint of accent."

"Where do you call home?" the woman asked.

"Thrace," Leandros told them.

"You told them where you were from, even though you had just met them?" I interrupted.

"I did, though I did not share the name of my tribe with them right away, uncertain who I could trust now that Zita's family had found your mother and I."

I nodded and allowed him to continue.

"What brought you and Zita so far south?" the man asked.

Leandros hesitated, knowing he could not tell them the true reason they had fled, or the path they had taken when they left the north.

"Zita and I fell deeply in love, but her family did not approve of our being together so, we left the tribe. We travelled from Thrace to Sparta through Macedonia, Thessaly, Boeotia and the Peloponnese until the travelling became too much for Zita and we found comfortable lodgings in Xirokambi. Our daughter arrived last night and soon after, Zita's family found us. Zita sent me away to save us both, urging me to keep Skylar from her family's wicked influence."

"Did they question you on what you meant?" I interrupted again.

"No, they just listened, offering words of comfort as I wept for my lost love and spoke of the fire that claimed her life and destroyed the house we were staying at."

"Cleomenes knows of the fire; it destroyed the entire village. He spoke briefly of it when I was with him. The town is now mostly abandoned."

Father nodded. "I heard there was nothing left when they were finished there."

"I can only imagine," I murmured. "Please go on."

"The loss you have endured this night is indeed cruel, but you must look to the future, for you and your daughter. You shall join us at our home and be provided with all you require," the woman said.

"What do they call you?" the man added as he approached.

"My name is Leandros."

"Well, Leandros of Thrace, allow me to introduce myself and my wife. I am King Anaxandridas of Sparta, of the royal Agiad line, and this is Queen Anassa."

Leandros bowed as well as he could with his daughter in his arms, his eyes finding his feet. "King Anaxandridas, Queen Anassa, it is an honor. I shall willingly provide you with the gift you desire in exchange for honey-sweetened wine for my daughter, and food and a soft bed for me."

"Do you not wish to know what we ask of you before you so quickly agree?" the king asked, putting his hand on Leandros' shoulder.

Leandros raised his eyes, straightening as he did so. "If it pleases you to speak of it now, then I shall be glad to hear it."

"It pleases me," Anaxandridas nodded. "My wife and I find ourselves in an unusual position. Please, sit," he said, indicating a long stone near the altar. Leandros did so, the king and queen joining him, one on either side. "For many winters we attempted to conceive a child, but to no avail. The healers told us that my wife was barren. The five ephors whom hold council with me, urged me to set aside my queen and take another wife, one who would provide me with the sons I desired. But I love my Anassa, much as I see you loved your Zita, and I told them I would not set her aside. They held great meetings to discuss what was to be done, finally allowing me to take another wife without setting Anassa aside."

The queen took up the story. "Shortly after, Anaxandridas and his second wife produced a son, Cleomenes, who shall take the throne when Anaxandridas passes into the Underworld. I did not begrudge him that, but I too sought another lover for comfort when Anaxandridas was with his second wife. Within a winter of Cleomenes being born, I also bore a son, Dorieus."

"Dorieus' father was killed shortly after his birth, so I raise him as my own, as I shall any subsequent children Anassa has."

"And I do the same for Cleomenes, though everyone knows I am not his birth mother. And now we must ask you of the gift we seek ..."

Leandros said nothing, though he believed he knew what the king and queen of Sparta sought from him – they wished to purchase his daughter. He knew if they asked it of him, he would decline their offer, and he did not believe they were denied their wishes very often.

"My wife yearns for a daughter and, as you have already created one with your Zita, we believe you can provide one for us," Anaxandridas said.

"In what manner would you have me do that?" Leandros managed, keeping his voice even.

"Not in the manner I am certain you are imagining," the king replied with a smile. "We can see how devoted you already are to your daughter and we do not wish to see the two of you separated. So, we would ask that you lay with my wife and put the child she so desires in her belly."

Leandros took a deep breath. It was not the request he had expected, but it did not cause any relief. He had barely begun to mourn Zita's loss. How could he possibly give himself to another woman and bear her a child so soon?

"I thank you for your words and ... I do not wish to offend, but I cannot give you what you want. My heart belongs to another and I mourn for her today, as I shall for many days yet. I am flattered for the offer, but fear that I would disappoint you in my inability to perform what is required to give you a daughter." Leandros wearily pushed himself to his feet. "Besides, why would you wish to lay with a Thracian tribesman? Why not one of your royal guards or a high ranking citizen of Sparta instead?"

"Those men would be more than willing, I assure you, but it is not them that I desire," the queen answered.

"You desire me?" Leandros echoed, a frown crinkling his forehead. "Yes."

"Again, I do not wish to offend you, Queen Anassa, but we have only just met, how is it that you desire me so already?"

Anassa stood also and put her hand on his chest as she replied. "I see that you have a kind heart, Leandros. A loyal heart. One that loves deeply, protecting those you must at any cost. You are strong and do not shy away from difficult decisions you must make, yet I see you war with yourself about what to do. Those are important traits and I would be proud to bring a daughter into this world that possessed the same."

"I cannot."

Anaxandridas joined them, taking a dagger from beneath his chiton and holding it at Leandros' throat. "Your refusal would disappoint my queen, and when my queen is disappointed, it angers me. I have been known to deal harshly with those who have denied her of any wish."

"My intention is not to disappoint or enrage either of you, King Anaxandridas, but can you not appreciate my reluctance in carrying out such an act?"

"I cannot. Do you know how many soldiers or citizens or slaves in Sparta desire the affections of the queen? Do you know the lengths they would go to for the chance to spend just one evening with her?"

"And I am honored that you would gift her to me in return for mere food and shelter for my child and me, but ... as I said; I cannot."

"Then perhaps we shall take your precious child instead. She is but a day old, she would not remember you, or her mother," Anaxandridas growled.

"I shall not allow you to take her from me. You shall not reach your house alive," Leandros told him, anger and fear driving his words.

The king laughed, removing the dagger from Leandros' throat. "And how does a dead man stop a king? My guards wait for us outside and would have you greeting Hades before you could lay a hand on me."

"Please Leandros, lay with me one night," the queen interrupted, standing between the two men. "Our daughter shall grow to be beautiful and strong. She shall possess your kind and loyal heart. She shall never want for food or coin. She shall be Princess of Sparta. Revered. Loved. Educated. Do you not wish for such an honor? Would you not wish it for the babe in your arms also?"

Leandros looked down to his daughter before replying. "Skylar shall have everything I can provide for her and it shall be enough. Wherever we go, wherever we settle, I shall teach her all that I know. She shall not be brought up as a Spartan or an Athenian. She shall have the choice of who she wants to be; educated, proficient in driving chariots or a citizen's wife whose house she tends with care and love, gifting him with many children."

The king brought the dagger back to Leandros' neck. "You hold bold dreams for her, but none of them shall come to pass unless you agree to satisfy my wife."

Leandros met the eyes of both Anaxandridas and Anassa before dropping them to the sleeping baby in his arms. The dagger pushed against his skin, cold and deadly. He had promised Zita he would protect Skylar. He had promised he would always be there for her. He could not fail. He knew what he must do.

He raised his eyes to meet the king's. "I shall lay with the queen for one night. But you must give me your word that after it is done, my daughter and I shall be free to leave your home, and Sparta, if I choose. You shall not pursue us, for I shall have done as you ask."

Anaxandridas smiled and lowered the dagger again. "I give you my word," he promised.

"The following evening after I had slept, eaten and settled you with Anassa's midwife, I went to the queen's room. I imagine you are appalled that I so quickly returned to another's bedroom when your mother was so soon taken from us b–"

"I understand," I told him, holding his gaze. I knew only too well what it was to want one person, and yet seek relief with another. My own actions had almost destroyed the budding relationship between Alexis and myself.

He held my stare, nodding in return. "I remained with Anassa for two days, with no one but the two of us in that room. We were not … intimate the entire time. We spent the first day just talking. She asked me of your mother, what I loved most about her, what had first drawn me to her. Anassa knew I felt that to be with her was a betrayal to Zita, and she did her best to set my mind at ease. I did not tell her everything about Zita, of course, though the questions she asked me I could answer without speaking of the Keres or how she had truly died.

"You were well cared for in my absence, you slept most of the time anyway, but when you woke, you were given the honey-sweetened wine Anassa had promised. Apparently, Cleomenes and Dorieus were quite taken with you – believing their mother had birthed them a baby sister, which is why she remained in her chambers – recovering."

"Perhaps, had my mother not been a Ker, it would have been easy for you to leave me there," I murmured.

"We are both well aware that children are sometimes left with others to be brought up. But for me, Ker heritage or not, I could *never* have left you behind."

"For which I am ever grateful," I smiled. He opened his arms and I crossed to him, wrapping my arms around his waist and allowing him to engulf me in his larger frame.

Father placed a kiss on the top of my head. "Anassa and I spoke of many things while we were together in that room; the mountains in Thrace, what my hopes were for you when you grew. And strangely, the more we spoke, the closer I felt to you, even though we were separated by walls and rooms. Healers speak of parental bonds only being formed with closeness and contact, but I felt our connection even away from you."

"It has not appeared to hinder our ability to be close with one another," I noted with a laugh.

Father chuckled as well, releasing me. "No indeed," he agreed.

"So I gather that you and Anassa were together eventually, and the result was Leonidas?"

"Yes, when there were no more words to be said between us in the dark candlemarks of the second day, we were together."

"Did you remain to find out if you had put a child inside her, just as she and Anaxandridas wanted?"

"No, I took you and began the nomadic lifestyle we had until we found ourselves here in Trachis. I heard she was with child again of course, and remained in towns around the Peloponnese until I heard Leonidas had been born. It was not the daughter they hoped for, but I heard no reports of abandonment of the child, at which point I expanded our travels to include Argolis and the eastern harbors, which your mother and I had not visited after we left Thrace."

"So, when we met Cleomenes and he told us of his mother's barrenness, it was not a new story to you?"

"No, though I did not want it known then. I was too afraid that if I admitted I had once been in Sparta, that Leonidas' heritage would be exposed. You and I had already heard many rumors of King's Cleomenes' sanity and the falling out with one of his broth–"

"Which was not true," I cut in, quickly recounting what Cleomenes had told me of his and Dorieus' misunderstood kinship, and of Dorieus' passing.

"Be that as it may, at the time, I could only rely on what I had heard up until then, and I did not want to put Leonidas in jeopardy if Cleomenes decided he was not a worthy half-brother."

I nodded. "You were always cautious what truths you shared with strangers, and with me," I murmured, though I gave him a grin.

"Winters of practice," he smiled back. "You do not appear upset I have never spoken of Leonidas, or told you he was your brother."

"No ... I am a little disappointed that we have grown without knowing of one another before now, but I understand your decision and want to keep him safe. The Spartan lifestyle has never been particularly forgiving for children who did not meet their parents' expectations. How many did we come across in the Taygetos Mountains simply abandoned for their sex, or some other perceived weakness?"

"Were it not for the people of the mountains, many more of those abandoned children would be dead now," Father nodded.

"Perhaps it is time you finally returned to Sparta and we all met. Cleomenes is a friend and I do not believe the truth of Leonidas' heritage would dissuade him from naming Leonidas as the future king if he believes it is in his people's best interests. Besides, for the moment it does not appear that Leonidas has any interest in the throne; he is a soldier, and a good one from what I saw, and heard."

"Perhaps it is time," Father agreed. "I shall consider it."

I only nodded in reply, understanding his need for time to make any such decision.

15

4th rising, Moon of Anthesterion

I stood on the northern balcony, overlooking the grassed area between the palace and the Melas River beyond where, as they were every morning, my father and Ava began their day together. I was overdue at the barracks, but I yearned for just a little longer alone in the early morning quietness to enjoy the pleasant temperature and the light breeze that lifted the hair from my shoulders. Normally I was not so eager to remain from Moeris and the soldiers but today, for reasons I could not understand, I was unsettled and the thought of expending that sort of energy to dispense with the unease did not hold any appeal.

My thoughts turned instead to how Trachis was a unique town, not just from our army's point of view, or my acceptance into or being allowed charge of it, but of how King Agrias sought to integrate many ways into his rule. He had begun doing so before my father and I arrived, but now it was far more obvious. He had not completely turned his back on his home of Macedonia, though his allegiance to his old gods and customs had diminished in the winters since we had arrived, and since we had visited his brother, Amyntas.

I had made the journey to Macedonia twice; once not long after Ava was born, the other when Amyntas officially named his son, Alexander, as heir to the Macedonian throne two winters ago. Melina did not want to visit, given that her own first child had been named Alexander; a truth known to her husband's kin. Agrias insisted she accompany the rest of us – to show strength where others would expect weakness. To her credit, she held herself well during the visit, no doubt aided by the obviousness that the man named Alexander appeared in no way similar to her dead boy.

Agrias had had his own misgivings about attending his brother's home, though he knew it important to confirm in person that he did not intend to challenge his nephew for the throne. There were those within the Macedonian King's council who wished to hear Agrias speak the words for themselves and judge his truthfulness. Agrias' actions – just as Melina's – had been nothing but respectful and truthful. In all, the visit with Agrias' kin was relatively short and Agrias had taken much pleasure in showing me the Diplos waterfall he had spoken of ten winters before, joining me in jumping from its dizzying height, the two of us alarming his queen and my princess alike.

The knowledge Father and I had brought with us about the Athenian Greeks and their learned (and often spirited) debates, plays and political customs, along with the Spartan training and discipline made for long discussions and questions about what would work best for Trachis and its people. There were few of my father's customs from Thrace that Agrias regarded as worthy, and Father did not disagree with him, still the king always had questions about the fierce tribe my father had once called home, and would have been happy to acknowledge them if my father wished it.

With so much history and oft-spoken of stories, Ava had grown with a mixture of all those cultures, and was not made or expected to adhere to one set of rules or customs. We all agreed that giving her such a wide variety of knowledge could only assist when the day arrived that Agrias, Melina, Alexis and myself had all passed into the Underworld, and she sat on the throne of Trachis as queen.

I was lost in my thoughts when Alexis' cool fingers slipped into mine. I started, my other hand automatically going to the pommel of my sword.

"Apologies, I did not mean to startle you," she murmured.

"Perhaps I am getting old, for I did not feel your presence as I always have, Princess."

"I cannot imagine that to be the truth," she grinned, turning her face to capture the first light. "It appears you have much on your mind. Were you plagued with unpleasant dreams again during the dark candlemarks?"

"No. I do not know what saw me awake so early," I replied, lifting her chin and placing a gentle kiss against her lips.

"If you were not supposed to be at the barracks, I would suggest we go to the hot springs and forget everyone and everything else for the morning."

"And I would have no hesitation in taking you up on that offer, I assure you of that," I sighed. "But you speak true, I should go to the men. I can only imagine the teasing they would afford me if I was as late to training as my father always is," I replied, my lips lifting in return.

"They would not dare question your reasons though," Alexis smirked.

"True, but I wonder what they would say if I told them it was the princess and our bed who kept me from their ranks …" I challenged, lifting an eyebrow.

Alexis colored slightly. "You would not speak of such with them. Would you?"

I laughed. "I have shared much about you with the men of the army, but those particular talents of yours do not enter my conversations with them. I am certain they have their opinions on it though."

Alexis leaned her head against my shoulder. "Gods, I do not wish to have them thinking of me in such a manner."

I wrapped my arms around her so the length of her body was pressed against mine. "I believe what is beneath your chiton has often been on their minds, as it is on mine, even when I have more important tasks at hand. Unfortunately for them they have never, and shall never, have it revealed to them," I said, attempting to keep the light tone in my voice.

"They shall not," Alexis agreed, pressing into me and pushing up onto her toes to claim my lips.

I reveled in the contact, wishing I could indeed miss the morning training session with the men and partake of the sweet pleasures my wife had to offer.

Reluctantly, I broke our contact. "I should join Moeris."

"Are you certain you cannot remain here a little longer?" she asked, sliding her fingers up my arm and over my cuirass, hooking them into the leather at my neck and pulling me forward, her tongue darting teasingly along and between my lips. I groaned, my hold at the small of her back tightening as I returned her fevered touches.

"Perhaps there is a more private area you would wish to make such displays," a quiet voice advised.

I loosened my grip on Alexis and faced Melina. "Perhaps there is," I acknowledged, inclining my head to her.

"Good morning, Mother," Alexis added. "We were ju–"

The queen held up her hand. "I need no explanation. It is pleasing to see the love you still have for one another after so many winters."

"It shall not change, no matter how long we are in this world," I assured her, holding her gaze with just a hint of defiance.

Melina nodded. "I understand. When one finds themselves with such powerful feelings, there are none who can change that."

"Indeed," I agreed.

"Perhaps it is time I allowed you to get to the barracks," Alexis said.

My grip tightened briefly again around her waist and I leaned in so only she would hear my next words. "Not a chance, Princess. Meet me at our chambers and finish what you began," I growled.

She only nodded in reply, her cheeks darkening once again. She did not meet her mother's eye as she passed, but managed to mumble that she and Ava would see her later in the morning for their visit to the agora and Melina's parents in town. I chuckled as the queen joined me.

"I see you can still bring a blush to my daughter's face when the mood strikes you," she noted.

"Indeed," I agreed again. I turned back towards the river, leaning my elbows on the top of the railing. "Was there something you wished to speak to me about?"

"Not at all, I was simply intending to take my morning walk when I came across the two of you."

I nodded, but said nothing, my daughter's laughter drifting on the breeze to us as my father did something particularly amusing in the water.

"Well?" Melina asked after a long moment. I met her gaze, an eyebrow raised as my own question. "Are you not supposed to be meeting my daughter somewhere? I cannot imagine the two of you would have keep hands from one another for much longer, had I not interrupted you."

"Er …"

She laughed and waved me away. "Go, go. I am surprised you have remained here as calmly as you have so far. Then again, restraint has often been your strength when it comes to Alexis and your feelings for her … for a time anyway."

Needing no further encouragement, I pushed off the railing, nodding hastily in Melina's direction and heading back through the walkway to the room Alexis and I shared.

Pushing the door shut behind me, I took in the sight of Alexis waiting for me on the bed – naked except for the slices of fig arranged in a line from her navel to her chin. I grinned, stalking across the room and tugging impatiently at the ties of my cuirass, pulling it over my head and dropping it to the ground without care for where it landed. Tumbling to the floor to join it barely a moment later, was my sword and tunic.

"What took you so long?" Alexis asked with a grin.

"Nothing important," I shrugged. "But it appears you found a way to occupy yourself until I arrived," I noted, reaching the bed.

I ran a hand up her leg, my tongue tracing a delicate line where my fingers had just been. Reaching the first of the fruit, I snatched it up between my lips and bit down, enjoying the sweetness and crunchy seeds within.

"Mm. Delicious," I murmured.

"You would prefer to eat?" Alexis pouted.

I smirked, sliding higher and taking the next fig from her stomach, offering it to her from between my teeth. She took it willingly, her lips brushing mine.

"Never, though it is important to be well fed before attempting physical pursuits," I assured her.

"Is it?" she asked, having finished the slice already.

"Oh yes." I leant down, cupping her cheek in my palm and kissing her firmly, my thigh sliding between hers.

"The figs," Alexis murmured, as we parted.

I slid my hand across her body, scattering the fruit onto the bed, and the floor beyond. "What figs?" I asked, my fingers finding the hardened skin of her nipple to distract her with instead.

"Oh … Gods. I am glad you suggested returning to our room," she managed, her back arching as I increased the pressure at her chest.

"Me too," I agreed, my lips taking over.

Alexis tangled a hand in my hair as my own began a tantalizing journey lower. Her hips lifted in response and my thighs moistened as I felt her gathered heat and wetness.

"Remind me to miss training more often," I drawled, nipping at Alexis' neck, my fingers working to draw her towards her release.

"Mmm. Definitely," she agreed.

16

LEANDROS
Melas River

Leandros stood thigh-deep in the dark, gently running water of the Melas River. Ava sat on the bank nearby, unwilling to get into the cold unless it was absolutely necessary. She had never been fond of the chilly temperature of the rivers around Trachis, preferring the hot springs to the south – unless of course the day was particularly hot and she needed to cool down after training with Philo or sparring with Nikomachos. Leandros though had always been able to coax her into the water in the summer, and taught her his method for catching fish. She was quite skilled at it already, and he knew that one day she would be better even than him. She just had to block the cold from her mind and concentrate on watching the fish she sought to catch.

They had been at the river almost three candlemarks already, arriving by torchlight before Eos' pale dawn greeted them. The pile of fish beside Ava attested to Leandros' skill, and the grin on his granddaughter's face proved how much she enjoyed their early morning time together. Their catches would be cleaned and prepared by Hesper in the palace kitchens when they were done. It did not matter how much, or how little, they caught each day for whatever could not be used in the palace went to the barracks or the townspeople.

Leandros crouched lower in the water, his hands outstretched in a familiar gesture. He could see the long fish approaching, though it would be a few moments until it reached him. His head remained still, but his eyes found Ava's. She grinned and he winked at her, returning his gaze to his prey. He watched the fish swim closer, realizing that they had caught a lot more fish than usual. He leaned his head to the side as he considered the idea. It was not that there were more in the water than usual. He realized that Ava had simply not scared as many away with her laughter as he made his preparations. The child was not preoccupied or saddened by anything as far as he could tell. Perhaps it was merely that she was getting older.

"Papou, you missed it," she cried, jumping up from her place on the bank and pointing to the fish that swam past him.

Cursing under his breath at his distraction, he leapt sideways, hands outstretched in desperation. His fingers curled around the fish's tail and he tightened his grip, fighting with the slippery beast as he attempted to get better purchase. Finally he had it by both stomach and fin and he held it aloft in triumph. Ava laughed and laughed, falling back into the grass as he threw the long, whiskery fish up next to her.

"Papou, you almost allowed it to get past you," she said when her laughter had subsided.

Leandros waded over, a smile lighting his own face. "Perhaps I wished to test myself a little this morning. We have caught so many so easily already," he replied, pulling himself out onto the bank and wiping his hands on his tunic.

"You did not, you were not paying attention," she corrected him, placing the newest addition on top of the others.

"Perhaps you speak true, my darling. What do you say we take what we have here and show Bion?"

Ava nodded, holding out her arms for Leandros to place four of the larger fish on top. He gathered up the rest, placing his fingers inside the gaping mouths and slipping his feet into his sandals.

Though it was faster to return to the palace across the grassy area below the northern balcony, Ava and Leandros always took the longer route through the town of Trachis so they could compare their catches to the fishermen at the agora. Some of the men fished off the rocks below the west gate of the Pass of Thermopylae, while others – Bion included – took their simple fishing vessels into the deeper waters. Bion was a close friend of Ophelos', which is how Leandros and Ava had come to know him, and the competition of their daily catches began.

"You are late today, friend," Bion called as Leandros and Ava approached.

"There were so many fish to be had. Was it not true for you also?" Leandros replied.

"About the same as most mornings," Bion replied with a shrug. "Do you have a moment to speak on another matter before you leave?"

"Of course, what is it?"

"Perhaps the little one could run along to her kin?" Bion said, pointing to Ophelos' wine stand fifteen or so stalls along.

"Whatever you have to say to Papou, you may say to me," Ava insisted before Leandros had the chance to respond. Her chin lifted in challenge of the older man and a bemused grin passed between the two men. Leandros placed a hand on Ava's shoulder and motioned for Bion to speak.

Bion smiled as well, not at all offended, but rather charmed by the fire in the young girl. "Very well. On my return this morning as Helios lit the sky for us, I noticed a boat between our shores and the island of Euboea. A trireme."

"Did you recognize it?" Leandros asked.

"It is not a Greek ship. It bears weapons and shields that mark them as Persian."

At the last word, Leandros stiffened, his grip tightening slightly on Ava's shoulder.

"Papou?" she asked.

Leandros forced himself to relax his hand and maintain a calm set to his face before he looked at her. "Take the fish you have to Aspasia. I shall fetch you from there soon."

"But, Papou," the girl began.

"Go," he said, forcefully but not unkindly.

Ava recognized the tone, though he did not use it with her often. She nodded once to show she understood and would do as he asked. Re-adjusting the fish in her arms, she headed off towards her great-grandparents' home, where Nasrin and Leandros also lived.

"Show me," Leandros ordered when he was satisfied that Ava had reached the house.

Bion nodded in reply, directing his son to watch the stall while he was gone, the young man taking the fish from Leandros and setting it with their own.

"Did you see anyone aboard?" Leandros asked as they walked.

"No, though as I said, it was still early. They were not there when Helios left us yesterday, so perhaps they still slumbered from their journey?"

"Perhaps," Leandros agreed, his mind searching for any possible reason why Persians would be in the Malian Gulf at all.

It had been less than a moon since Cleomenes had made the decision not to assist Aristagoras against Darius. Had the foolish Milesian been captured and spoken of Trachis' connection to the Spartan King in order to make himself appear more useful to his enemy?

"There. You see it?" Bion asked when they reached the beach. Leandros nodded in reply, instantly finding the larger boat amongst the fishing vessels. "What do you think they are doing here?" Bion asked.

"I cannot imagine," Leandros replied, placing a hand on the other man's shoulder. "But I must take the news to Moeris and Skylar. And Agrias. Keep an eye out for strangers in the market and send word of them to the barracks."

"Of course," Bion dipped his chin.

Leandros nodded again to the fisherman, hurrying back through the crowded, noisy streets of the agora, collecting his fish and Ava on the way back to the palace.

Having returned Ava to Alexis, Leandros went to the barracks, only weakly acknowledging the greetings and good natured teasing about his late attendance from the older men. Skylar looked up at the sound of his name, calling a halt to the young man who stood with her, his sword and shield coated with dust, attesting to his less than successful morning's work.

Skylar often worked with the newest members of the army, ensuring they learned the correct techniques from the outset, and that their hearts truly yearned for a place amongst the ranks, rather than merely attempting to bolster the numbers. Sander and Kleitos usually assisted her, but as the two of them were with Hektor and Demosthenes in the east, she shouldered the task alone.

A number of boys not yet old enough to join the soldiers' ranks watched Skylar and the ephebes from the doorways leading to the barracks. Leandros recognized Kleitos' younger brother, Lysistratos, amongst them. Kleitos had trained harder than ever before this past winter, knowing his younger sibling was to join in a few winters' time and not wanting to be shown up when he did. Lysistratos was a natural with sword and shield – he, Ava and Nikomachos often scrapping together. The two boys would enter the army together the same spring, and perhaps Ava would press for a position beside them when she reached eighteen winters. Skylar and Alexis had never said she could *not* join, though neither had they indicated that she could or would. It had not come up for serious discussion as yet.

Leandros motioned Skylar over and they scooped cups of fresh water out of the barrel before joining Moeris where he stood nearby, watching two others spar.

"There is a Persian boat anchored offshore between the beach and Euboea," Leandros told them without preamble.

"Persian?" Moeris asked.

"Are you certain?" Skylar responded at the same time.

He nodded to them both. "I saw it with my own eyes."

"Do we know what they want?" Skylar asked.

"No, though I doubt their presence here can mean anything good."

Skylar frowned, drawing a deep breath and expelling it all the way out before she spoke again. "Do you believe Aristagoras is to blame for their arrival? Or perhaps our involvement at Naxos?"

"I wondered the same," Leandros replied. "But I cannot be certain. We cannot know unless we engage them."

"We have not heard any reports from Kleitos and Sander, perhaps they are being held aboard – the Persians expecting payment in exchange for their return?" Moeris mused.

Leandros shrugged. "Perhaps, but as far as we know, the Persians have not left their ship, which I would have expected if they wished to speak terms with us."

"Then I shall go and find out what they want," Skylar nodded.

"No," Leandros said, shaking his head. "Nasrin has taught me some of their language. I shall go."

"Allow me to join you then," she countered.

Again he denied her. "I do not intend to engage them in conversation. At least not until we know their intentions. I need only hear what they are saying amongst themselves."

"Depending on what you overhear, it may not be conversations we need to have with them," Moeris murmured.

"You may well speak the truth," Leandros agreed.

"I do not approve of you going alone," Skylar said.

"If I was in your position, I am not certain I would be either. But you understand it is the best way to find out what we need to. One person is easier to conceal than two."

Skylar paused a long moment before nodding in reply.

"How long until you have something to report?" Moeris asked.

Leandros lifted a shoulder. "I shall take a fishing boat some of the way then swim the remainder. So … perhaps with the beginning of the new day at sundown."

"Very well," Moeris said with a curt nod. "If we do not see you before, we shall take as many men as one of the fishing boats can carry and come for you. I shall have others remain on the beach until you return. If the Persian vessel leaves before you come ashore again, we shall not hesitate to pursue."

"Understood," Leandros nodded, the two men gripping forearms in agreement.

"Be safe," Skylar added, taking her father's arm and squeezing.

"I shall. Do not worry."

"I cannot make such a promise but I trust in your decision."

"Ensure Thaddeus is aware of the situation should Agrias, Melina and the rest of the royal family be required to be taken to safety. I would include you in that number, but I know you shall want to be with the soldiers if defense is required," Leandros said, holding Skylar's forearm longer than was necessary.

"I may be considered their kin, but I shall always be a warrior first," she told him.

"I know," he agreed.

The three of them nodded to one another, Leandros heading back into town to gather weapons and tell Nasrin of what he had learned, the other two returning to training.

17

Leandros anchored the small boat, watching for soldiers or slaves on the Persian vessel. It was similar to the Athenian triremes he had seen in the south with two rows of oars, one above the other; eighty-five on each side. He wondered if it were soldiers or slaves who propelled the boat, but with no one at all on the upper deck, it was impossible to know. His eyes fell on the shields propped against the sides; they were tall rather than round and though they would protect the entirety of one side of the body, they appeared to be made only of wood, rather than bronze.

As the candlemark drew on, the sound of voices reached Leandros. Wanting to appear as non-threatening as possible should he need to approach the men, he removed his sword and placed it beneath the seat, his cuirass following it. Wearing only his tunic and sandals, Leandros slipped into the water, keeping his strokes through the coolness as quiet as possible. He reached the bobbing wood, the voices clearer there, and he raised his brows as they spoke in perfect Greek, with no hint of accent or a Persian word.

"Why must we wait? We know where he is. We understand your plan. We should put it into action."

"Do not question me again, unless you wish to find yourself impaled on the end of *my* sword rather than any soldier you face here."

There was something vaguely familiar about the second voice but Leandros could not place it for the moment. He pulled himself up to one of the oar holes. Six soldiers were clustered together, their legs and heads wrapped in bright yellow cloth, more colored material forming sleeves at the arm holes and beneath their white chest pieces. The white cuirasses were familiar to Leandros; he had faced Persian soldiers in Naxos who wore the same. They were not effective against Greek sword and spear. Over the top of it all was another bright red length of material, worn akin to the himations of the Spartan army, and pinned at one shoulder. Their spears were strapped to their backs, in easy reach if required, yet out of the way enough to move about easily.

Leandros frowned again. They were dressed as Persians, yet clearly they were not. What were they doing here, and in such clothing? He altered his position at the oar, his eyes widening as he took in the form of Ares. As though sensing his presence, the God of War turned and Leandros released his grip and dropped into the water.

Through the quiet encasing his ears, he heard rushing footsteps across the wooden planks beside him and a number of commands. He dived deeper, determined to get as far away from the vessel as possible with the breath he held in his chest. When he broke the surface, he was still a fair distance from his own small boat and barely had time to draw a welcome gasp of air when the net hit him.

He drew in another quick breath and dove back beneath the waves, his attempts to reach the bottom of the Malian Gulf and elude the thick rope in vain as it snapped tight around him and prevented his escape. He was caught as though he was a fish in Bion's net; too large to fit through the tightly wound braids and too weak to simply tear them apart and free himself.

He could do nothing as he was pulled to the surface and dragged towards the boat. The soldiers hoisted him up the side none too carefully; his head hitting the wood several times on the way before he was dumped onto the deck.

"Welcome," Ares grinned, the soldiers freeing Leandros from the mesh.

He reached for the sword at his side, momentarily forgetting he was not carrying it. "Ares," he growled.

"You no longer refer to me as Thrax? You truly have left all your Thracian ways."

"It makes no difference what your name is; your presence can only mean trouble."

The God of War threw back his head and laughed. "Ah, I have missed our exchanges. And those with Skylar. Tell me, how is Ava? Well? Growing strongly as my blood pumps through her?"

"She has no more of your blood in her than she does the current Archon of Athens," Leandros replied.

Ares only shrugged, addressing the soldiers beside him. "Take him below." They nodded and hauled Leandros up, struggling to hold him as he writhed in their grip. Ares stepped forward and crashed his hand across Leandros' head with brutal force; his chin dropping to his chest as he was knocked unconscious.

*

Leandros came to sometime later, his head throbbing painfully. A lack of strong light outside his closed lids told him several candlemarks had passed. He opened his eyes, finding his right one stuck slightly by what he could only assume was dried blood; the left opening far easier. He attempted to lift his hand to the wound, but his hands and feet were ensnared in more thick rope, his escape prevented by the other end's attachment to the nearest rower's bench.

"Ah, finally you awaken," Ares drawled, pushing off the side of the boat.

"There are soldiers on the beach. They wait for my report. If I do not return they shall come. Release me or find yourself faced with the army of Trachis," Leandros warned.

"Ha! You believe a small army of mortals are any match for my soldiers?" Ares laughed. With a wave of his hand, the God of War conjured a hundred soldiers in the same Persian clothing Leandros had seen earlier. The men crowded the hull, faces blank and unmoved by where they found themselves, or of the company they were in. "These men serve me without question, they live and die by the task I have set them. If I told one to kill another, they would, because I asked it of them. They live in my palace on Olympus and join battles beside mortals when I believe the cause great enough, and one faithful to my ways and beliefs prays for me to do so," Ares told him.

"The soldiers on the beach are capable. If your soldiers are not immortal, then our men can exploit their weaknesses and dispatch of them faster than you believe possible. It is what we teach them to do here in Trachis," Leandros countered.

"I am aware of much in Trachis, old man. Though what you do

with your army is of no interest to me. Not yet anyway. Besides, your soldiers shall get your report. And they shall remain on land, and far from this boat."

"Oh? How is that?" Leandros asked.

Ares grinned. He rolled his shoulders and stretched his neck from side to side. Leandros could only stare, open-mouthed as one by one, the God of War's features turned into his own; body, face, clothing. If he had not witnessed the change personally, he would never have known that the man in front of him was not a Thracian-born warrior with the name of Leandros.

"Wha–? How?" he stammered.

Ares smiled again and shrugged. "There is little I cannot do if I wish to. I am a god after all."

Leandros' question had not *truly* needed an answer, but it appeared Ares could not help himself. *Still as arrogant as ever*, Leandros silently thought.

"Now you understand how your words shall meet the soldiers of Trachis' ears."

Leandros could only nod. There was no doubt the soldiers on the beach would be no wiser when Ares appeared to them. He had to break free of his bindings and escape before the God of War learned he was gone, because if he found out, Leandros knew he would not reach the town before Ares did. No mortal could.

"When I speak with your men on the beach and convince them there is no threat, my men shall be amongst the townspeople – and they too shall rally no defense against foreign soldiers."

"What trick do you have to ensure that?" Leandros asked, frowning.

Ares grinned and waved his hand again, the soldiers around them shimmering momentarily. When they became clear again, each face was that of a townsperson or soldier Leandros recognized. He gasped; his lover was among them. Ares' grin widened.

"Those ... people," Leandros managed. "Do they still live?" Ares said nothing and Leandros tore his gaze from Nasrin's to meet the god's. "Do they live?" he repeated.

"They do – just as you do, even though I am able to take your form. Though if you wish it to be otherwise ..." Ares taunted.

Leandros fought against his restraints once again. Ares appeared unconcerned, his smile firmly in place as he folded his arms across his chest.

"They shall walk amongst those they know, though they have orders to immediately make their way to the palace."

"Why?"

"Oh I believe you know who they seek there … and once they pass through the portico, the faces you see before you now shall simply disappear, replaced with the yellow caps and cloth covered bodies of Persian soldiers. You and I both know there are those in Trachis who already despise or fear those from the east. And after tonight there shall be one whose heart beats with special hatred for the men who destroyed the idyllic life she has known thus far."

"Ava," Leandros whispered. "Ares, please, do not do this."

"You should know by now that your pathetic pleading falls upon deaf ears where I am concerned. Ava is my Chosen One and the events in the dark of this particular night shall propel her towards the great fate which awaits her at my side."

"Plea—"

"I too shall appear as a Persian when my Chosen One sees me," Ares cut over him. A second change went over the God of War. Leandros blinked. Ares was one of them. He would fool everyone into believing the Persians had arrived. *Ava* would believe that Persian soldiers were responsible for whatever it was Ares had in mind.

Leandros shivered. He could only imagine what those actions would consist of. He *must* escape the boat and warn everyone. He bucked against the ropes again. Again they held him in place, although the one at his right wrist gave ever so slightly.

"Do not make me send you to Hypnos' realm again," Ares warned.

Leandros continued to wriggle his hand in the rope. "It is the only way you can ensure I remain here," he growled.

"As you wish," Ares said with another shrug. "It is time I set in motion the events which shall begin my Chosen One's lust for revenge and death."

"You shall not succeed," Leandros promised.

Ares only laughed in reply. "You cannot stop me, old man." He grabbed a spear from the nearest soldier. Leandros ducked, but not before the thick wood struck him across the temple; placing him in the God of Sleep's clutches once again.

18

ARES
5th rising, Moon of Anthesterion

One of the soldiers the mortal had spoken of held his torch up higher, making out the small boat approaching the beach.

"He returns," he said to his companions.

Ares grinned, pulling strongly on the oars as the vessel crested a small wave, taking him towards the sand even quicker. He raised a hand in response.

"What news have you?" the first man asked, hauling the boat up and offering his hand to the older man.

"We have no reason to fear or engage the men in the anchored boat," Ares replied, his voice a perfect mimic of the Thracian's.

"Who are they?"

"Inexperienced sailors from Persia. Part of their training under Darius is to navigate themselves to an ally across the seas." The lie rolled easily off the god's tongue, the soldiers believing every word without question. "They are on their way to King Agrias' brother – Amyntas – in Macedonia. A combination of inexperience and meeting a nasty storm sees them far from their intended destination."

"They have been in the harbor all day, when are they leaving?"

"Why did they not come ashore to request assistance or seek directions?" questioned a second soldier before Ares could reply to the first.

"They are not allowed to ask for aid. Though if the information is given freely – such as I provided to them – they can use the knowledge to see them to their destination."

The men nodded and Ares grinned with Leandros' lips, the first man clapping him on the shoulder as he spoke again. "Come, we should return to the barracks and you can tell Moeris what you learned."

The second soldier nodded in agreement and reached into the boat, taking out Leandros' cuirass and handing it to him.

Ares took the leather and stepped out of the soldier's reach. "You go on ahead. I must go to the palace; Skylar is there and if I know her, she shall be impatiently waiting for me."

"Of course," the soldiers nodded again. We shall gather the rest of the men from the beach and pass your words onto Moeris."

"Good," Ares nodded.

The sun had dipped low enough that the beach was shrouded in darkness when the soldiers took the torches and moved away. Without their light highlighting the small boat, or the god pretending to be a mortal, Ares dropped the armor back onto the bench seat and with a final smirk, disappeared in a flash of light, not caring who may see the sudden illumination, or wonder at what it was.

19

I sat beneath the high window in our room, rubbing beeswax into my cuirass. Apart from helping to keep the leather supple and strong, if I suddenly found myself facing the Persians in the Malian Gulf, it would keep the water out. I hoped it would not come to that but I had a feeling that all was not as it should be in Trachis tonight. I had told Alexis of the boat in the Gulf, and that I hoped the fight would not come ashore, but I was not convinced that would be the case.

Ava sat at the small table in front of the mirror, Alexis brushing out her dark hair and speaking of days long past, her eyes alternating between the job at hand, and my face.

"Your Mumma has always been brave, even when she did not know me or know that I was the Princess of Trachis. She saved me from harm the first day we met, earning herself an injury our healer did not believe she would recover from. But she was so strong and determined that she did. Ever since, she has always been near when I needed her. She still protects me, protects all of us – you and me and our entire town – when she travels with the soldiers to quell threats against our lands."

"Tell me of one time when she saved you," Ava asked.

Alexis smiled, catching my eye. "Perhaps tonight I shall tell you my favorite, though it is one you have heard many times before."

"Alexis," I grumbled.

"Please Mumma, allow her to speak of it, it is my favorite as well," Ava pleaded. I shook my head, but did not protest again, turning back to my task.

"It was soon after we had spoken of our love for one another," Alexis began. "The Illyrian warriors had arrived in Trachis, having joined with the Epirotes to take Trachis for themselves. An Epirote warrior named Melanthios stole me from the palace as Thaddeus was getting me and Grandmother Melina into hiding. Your Mumma came after us, rescuing me and killing Melanthios so he could never hurt me – or anyone else – ever again. She shall always be my hero for she has always saved me when I needed her to."

I shifted uncomfortably, the story still slightly bothering me, even after so many winters. I still remembered the joy and immense sense of power I had felt as I tortured and then killed Melanthios. It was so similar to when I used the amulet to kill the soldiers who had captured Alexis moons later, and I now believed it was Ares' influence running through me that day with Melanthios.

I set aside my cuirass and the beeswax, crossing to my girls. "I wish you would not speak of that particular day quite so often," I murmured, bending down and placing a kiss on Ava's forehead.

"I know," Alexis replied.

"But Mumma, I love hearing how heroic you are, it makes me proud," Ava added.

I mentally shook my head. "Thank you," I said, squeezing her shoulder. I straightened, placing a kiss on my wife's lips as well, before leaning close to speak quietly at her ear. "What happened then to you, what he did to you, still angers me. I feared that you would not forgive me for allowing you to be taken."

Alexis placed a hand on my arm as she replied. "I know, but we have overcome so much since. We are strong, we can face anything together."

"That may be true, but it does not change my feelings about that day." I withdrew, holding her gaze for a few long moments, knowing just how many hurdles we had faced – and overcome – together in the ensuring winters. Not least, the one that saw us gifted with the child in front of us now.

"We have shared many days, and nights, together since then, and I like to think of them often," she said, a suggestive smile lighting her face.

"Mmm, so do I," I agreed. I cupped her cheek and pressed my lips to hers again, savoring the taste and feel of her as I deepened our kiss. Alexis responded in kind, the hand on my arm sliding to my waist to draw me closer. My heart quickened and body heated when she slipped her tongue into my mouth and I groaned. Ava snickered, reminding me that Alexis and I were not alone. Yet.

Reluctantly I released Alexis, noting her darkened cheeks and rapidly rising and falling chest. "Yes you do," I grinned, giving her a look that suggested that what we had just begun was not finished. She swallowed and I turned my attention back to our daughter. "Come now, my little princess, it is time for your bath. You would not want your grandfather to mistake you for a fish in the morning." I hoisted her out of the chair. "With slimy, smelly skin, he would seek to grab you in his grasp and throw you up onto the bank with the rest of his catches," I added, tickling her.

Ava giggled and squirmed as Alexis grinned, setting aside the comb and collecting our daughter's clean tunic as she followed us to the bathing area.

20

Leandros released his hand from the thick rope, working quickly on the other side until it fell to the wooden floor of the lightly bobbing vessel. He jumped the nearest bench and emerged onto the deck. The small boat he had rowed out into the Gulf was gone; by Ares presumably, and he could only hope he would find it again when he reached the shore. If he was fortunate, his cuirass and sword would still be aboard and he was in no doubt he was going to need them when he reached the palace. Taking a deep breath, he dove into the water, stroking quickly and powerfully through the cold waves, desperate not to be too late to stop Ares in his plans.

Ares stood in the Throne Room of the palace of Trachis, having sent the rest of his men to surround the town. He knew he would not need more at the palace.

"Remember what I have told you. She is strong, and smart. Do not assume that mere muscle shall be able to hold her. Not what I have planned," Ares grinned at the four soldiers, who nodded their understanding.

The soldiers' faces were no longer cloaked as those of the Trachis townspeople, but as Persian warriors, just as he had told Leandros they would be when they passed through the portico. With short spears strapped to their backs and axes hooked into their

belts, they appeared Persian in every manner. Wicker shields were propped within easy reach against the walls, and one man held a bow, three arrows over his shoulder, should the rope the others held not be enough to contain the woman. Ares remained in his usual leather outfit, waiting until it was time for him to become a Persian as well. *Almost time.* He grinned again.

The faintest of noises reached my ears from the outer room. I turned my head, waiting for it to come again. A sword being tapped against the second bath perhaps? I passed the cloth I was holding to Alexis, my eyes finding the wooden door as she took over washing Ava's back. I straightened. It was not unusual for both rooms of the bathing area to be used at once. But the distinctive sound... what was it?

"What is it?" Alexis asked, clearly sensing the change in my demeanor.

"I do not know. Remain here," I replied, silently cursing that I had left my sword in our room. I stepped through the doorway, noting no one in the outer room. I closed the door behind me and made my way out of the bathing area altogether, beneath the veranda of the south side of the palace and towards the central chamber and my weapons. There was no one in the courtyard or in any of the doorways – the inhabitants of the palace either already in bed or not yet back from whatever revelry they found themselves enjoying.

I reached our rooms without incident and belted my sword at my waist. As I prepared to slide my cuirass over my head, a familiar voice spoke. "Miss me?"

I turned, wondering if perhaps I was already in Morpheus' realm and this was another dream. "Ares," I breathed. "What are you doing here?" Before I could draw my weapon, he was at my side, my sword removed from its sheath and my cuirass from my hands.

"It is time," was all he said, throwing my weapon and armor aside and wrapping an arm around my waist.

I felt the familiar pull as he took me wherever he intended. I attempted to speak, but could not, my eyes closing of their own desire as I fell into unconsciousness.

I woke to find myself in the Throne Room, my hands bound with thickly braided rope. Four Persian soldiers stood nearby, eyeing me coldly, their hands resting on the pommels of their swords. I tested the bonds, but they were secure. For now at least.

"You still wear my amulet – have you noticed any changes in it recently? Has it alerted you to the truth that my Chosen One is almost ready?"

"Of course not, and I only wear it so I know that you do not have it," I replied.

Ares laughed. "Do you truly believe that if I wanted it, I would not simply take it from you? You must excuse me for a moment," he suddenly said. "There is someone else who must join us here."

"Do not hurt her," I warned, dread flooding through me. I did not know if he spoke of Alexis or Ava, but feared for them both equally.

In a blinding flash of light, the God of War disappeared, his men remaining where they were without the slightest of flinches. He returned barely a moment later. With Alexis. She looked terrified, attempting to shrink away from the powerful grip of the god who held her tightly, his fingers turning the skin at her wrist white.

"Skylar," she murmured.

"I know," I nodded. "Where is Ava?" I demanded, turning my attention back to Ares. "What did you do to her? Did you harm her?"

"Of course not. She is the future. My future. The one I have waited for. She *is* my Chosen One," he replied, taking another length of rope.

"It is not true," Alexis murmured.

"The line of the Keres does not run through her, Ares. She is not what you think she is," I told him, struggling to free myself from the ropes.

"She has always been what I thought," Ares replied, completing the loops around Alexis' wrists. "The time has come, just as I told you when we found ourselves together in Morpheus' realm."

"They were real conversations?"

"Oh yes. I told you the time was coming. That soon she would be old enough to wield the amulet, just as you had."

"You speak no truth."

Ares grinned. "Ah, but I do. What I did not tell you though, was that I am certain she shall be able to use all four of the amulet's elements; fire, water, wind and earth."

"If *any* of that is true, then it is far too soon. You told me that with my half-mortal blood, you had to wait until I was nineteen winters old. With Ava being full mortal, the same applies, or perhaps you shall have to wait even longer."

"Or perhaps the power has been erased altogether with those changes?" Alexis ventured.

Ares laughed, patting Alexis' cheek gently. "If only it was that simple my dear Alexis."

"How can you be so certain it is not?" I asked.

"Because I would have felt the disturbance, and all I felt the night she was brought into this world, was power."

Leandros arrived at the barracks, tunic still dripping from the water of the Malian Gulf, his cuirass and sword positioned haphazardly over the top. Moeris and Thaddeus stood laughing together near the

barrel of water in the training area, a cup in each of their hands.

"Moeris," Leandros managed.

The smile on the named man's lips died when he caught sight of his friend. "Leandros, what is it? What is wrong?" he asked, the cup falling from his grasp.

"Persians. Ares," Leandros managed, falling to his knees to catch his breath.

"What? The men on the beach told me there was no reason for concern. That you told them of it yourself."

"It was not me. It was Ares. He has disguised his soldiers as townspeople, at least until they reach the palace. Then they shall appear as Persians. I cannot know for certain what he has planned but I know it has to do with Skylar and her family, possibly even Agrias and Melina."

Thaddeus knelt down, offering his cup to Leandros, who took it and drained it in one gulp. "I shall find the king and queen and take them somewhere safe," he said. "They were headed to bed last I spoke with them."

"Do not take them through the main entrance; that is the way Ares' men shall come from," Leandros advised.

"The northern balcony," Moeris suggested. "Go that way. Now." Thaddeus nodded, grabbing up his shield as he left.

"Rouse the soldiers and meet me at the portico. We need to brace the doors and defend the palace from the inside. I shall find Skylar, Alexis and Ava," Leandros said, pushing himself to his feet again, the fresh water having revived him somewhat.

"We shall be there momentarily," Moeris assured him, offering his arm. Leandros took it and they squeezed one another tightly.

I struggled in the restraints, feeling the left side loosen. "There was not a mark on her the night she was born. You know that," I insisted. "We were all there. You confirmed it yourself. There was nothing on her shoulder. She is *not* a Ker, she is *not* your Chosen One. You are lying."

"Am I?" Ares smirked. "Do you honestly believe I would be here now if Ava was not the one I had waited so long for?"

Alexis slumped against the wall, a whispered 'no' escaping her lips. I found her eyes and held them, shaking my head against his words. But was he telling the truth? Could Ava have that part of me? The part I did not want her to have, that I had been certain she did not have? It could not be so. Alexis and Thaddeus were the main parts of her, it was true that she carried some of my stubbornness and determination, but she displayed so many more of their qualities; kindness, compassion, gentleness. That was who she was, she was not a Ker. She could not be.

They have been gone a long time. Where are they? Ava could not simply wait there for them to return any longer. Dressing quickly in the fresh tunic her mother had brought for her, she crept from the bathing area, her still-damp hair leaving drops of water behind as she walked along the veranda. Voices carried to her from the Throne Room, one of them she was certain was her Mumma's. She crept in that direction, crouching behind the large statue of Artemis, the marble chilling her hands and thighs where they touched.

Ares cocked his head to the side and smiled. *My Chosen One is here. Good.* **A grin lifted one corner of his mouth.**

Ava shivered and gripped tighter to the goddess. The dim light showed her mothers, bound and guarded by four soldiers.

Ares turned to me, a smirk on his lips as his features changed from the familiar dark-haired and leather-clad god I had come to despise, to a shorter, battle-scarred Persian soldier. His hair was covered with dark yellow cloth and he wore rich red robes over the white chest piece. Terror forced me to tug again at the bindings at my wrists. My dark hair flew about as I struggled to free myself. Alexis remained huddled and frightened against the wall, her green eyes large in her pale face.

Ava knew the soldiers were Persian. Nasrin had spoken with her of the yellow material they wore on their legs. Why are they here? Does it have to do with Mumma's visit to Sparta?

Ares took a small knife from his waist and grabbed Alexis by the arm, dragging her away from the wall and to her feet. He stood behind her, the knife at her throat as he looked up at me again. My heart skipped a beat, I had seen Alexis held in that manner before, but that time it had been only a soldier that held her, not the God of War, and I did not have an amulet that would obey my command or a pair of wings I could call upon to free her this time. *Where is Father? Has he returned? Does he know Ares is here? Are he and Moeris forming a defensive attack at this very moment?*

"The child is old enough to know the truth," Ares said, breaking into my thoughts. "Things shall soon begin to happen to her, just as they did you. Would you have her go through it without explanation? Would you wait unt–?"

"She is not of the line. How many times must we speak of this? She has no mark. There is *no* connection with her," I insisted.

"She *is* the one I have waited for and it is time for you to decide; shall you teach her or must I force your hand?"

He took his knife from Alexis' throat, his other hand holding her chin still as he sliced a long line down her cheek. She whimpered and bit her lip, the pink skin turning white with the pressure, but she did not give him the satisfaction of crying out.

"Stop!" I commanded, finally freeing my right hand and landing a blow in the nearest Persian soldier's face. I heard a satisfying crack as his head whipped back with the force. The bow in his hand clattered to the ground and I scooped it up, reaching for the sharpened lengths at his shoulder.

"Sky, no, please," Alexis pleaded.

I left the arrows where they were, turning instead to Alexis as I replied. "After the last time he was here, I swore I would never allow him to hurt you or Ava. No matter what." I lashed out as a second Persian approached.

Ava frowned. The man with the knife has been here before?

My wild swing found only air as the soldier went low and rammed into me, knocking me to the ground, his weight pinning me in place. I lost my grip on the bow as I kicked and thrashed, two more soldiers approaching. One hauled me to my feet by my hair and held me tightly as the others re-bound my hands. Ares pushed Alexis into the hands of the soldier whose nose I had broken and grabbed me by the throat, lifting me off the ground.

"You shall do what I tell you to do, when I tell you to do it," he growled, the bow snapping beneath his boots.

"Go to Tartarus," I choked out.

I drew up my legs and kicked out, catching Ares in the stomach. He doubled over, gasping, and I fought with everything I had. Alexis was pleading with me, but her words were drowned out by the pounding of blood in my ears. I had to get the ropes off again. I had to save Alexis. I had to go back to the bathing area for Ava and we had to take her far from here. Far from Ares. Never stop moving. That was what my mother had told my father. It had worked for them until they stayed a moon in Xirokambi before my birth. It had worked for Father and me until we remained here in Trachis for too long. Ares and Dianthe may have known of me, but they had never appeared before that. It had to be the answer. We had to hide Ava from Ares and everything he represented.

Ares looked up, panting. "You shall regret that."

21

A res straightened again. "This night shall mark the beginning of all I have dreamed of. I knew before I came that you would never agree to teach Ava about her past. Oh, I hoped you would change your mind of course, though given our history, I did not hold much hope." His tone was almost conversational, but I watched him warily, preparing myself for his next move – and mine. "So, I have come up with another option." He picked his knife up from where it had fallen.

I had to keep him talking long enough to free my arms again. "Which is?"

He laughed. "If I told you that, it would not be a surprise, would it?"

I almost had them. Just another moment would see it so.

Leandros burst through the walkway from the barracks, his eyes finding his granddaughter behind the statue of Artemis in the courtyard garden. He ran, not game enough to call her name. As he neared, he glimpsed Skylar in the Throne Room, bound, but working furiously to break out of the ropes around her wrists. She faced the Persian soldier Leandros knew was Ares and his heart skipped as he saw he held Alexis.

Ares placed a hand on Alexis' shoulder, drawing the knife back with his other.

Leandros reached Ava and wrapped his arms around her; one hand across her mouth, the other over her eyes as he picked her up. Her body tensed, but he turned without hesitation, running back towards the barracks. Her obvious initial shock wore off and she squirmed in his grasp. He tightened his grip and she stopped her attempt to escape.

I could do nothing but watch as Ares plunged the knife into Alexis' stomach, my hands useless in their bindings.

Leandros passed through the walkway, turning right into the training ground of the barracks, puffs of dust billowing behind him as he ran.

"No!" I screamed.

Skylar's anguished cry carried on an echo from the walls of the palace and courtyard, reaching the running figure and the child in his arms without censure. Leandros' steps faltered and his chest heaved as he felt Alexis' sudden loss. He may have ensured Ava's silence and blindness so she was not witness to what Ares would do to her mother, but the sound of Skylar's voice would haunt her for many winters, as it would Leandros. He knew there was no denying the truth of that. He had to take Ava somewhere safe, and quickly. He needed to return and help Skylar defeat the God of War once and for all.

Alexis' face was frozen with surprise as Ares drew the knife from her stomach. Blood dripped from her mouth and her limbs remained rigid, not even going to the wound to attempt to stop the life from draining from her. She was dead where she stood.

"No, no, no!" I cried. I felt the sharp edge of the knife in every part of me. My world was fading as fast as the lifeblood of my beloved wife. I scratched madly at the ropes again. Finally they came loose and dropped to the ground. Too late. I was too late. I crossed to Alexis, shoving Ares aside and darting past him as Alexis slumped forward.

"Leave them," Ares' words reached me and the soldier who had stepped toward me halted.

With a silent command to his suddenly leaden legs, Leandros began to move again, running faster than before until he was clear of the barracks and onto the plain below. There were none of Ares' soldiers there. *Probably headed to the Throne Room,* he thought.

I should have seen it coming. I should have known he would use Alexis, that if he provoked me enough, he could end her life just to torture me. He knew how much she meant to me and I had played right into his hands. My child, my lover, they were my weaknesses. What I would do to protect them was central to his plan and I should have seen it.

Thaddeus emerged from the ramp of the northern balcony, pulling the king and queen behind him, their footsteps loud and fast, even on the short grass. Leandros headed directly for him.

"No, Alexis, no," I sobbed, hot tears staining my cheeks as I cradled her head in my lap. "I failed you so badly. I am sorry. So sorry. I love you." I repeated the words over and over as I brushed the hair from her face. I closed her eyes. I had lost her. For all her talk of me being her hero, in this moment I was not. I had lost the only woman I ever truly loved, the woman who had so easily broken through all my defenses with no more than a kind smile and her easy touches. Who had loved me so fiercely and remained convinced I would always protect her or come for her, no matter what. But I had not protected her as I had always promised. I had failed her and in the end she knew it. If we met in the Underworld, she would never forgive me. I did not deserve her to. But I would ask it of her. I still needed her forever and always.

"The Throne Room, Thaddeus. Go," Leandros told him, allowing him past before he thrust Ava into the queen's waiting arms.

"Take her to your father's house in town, you should be safe there. Do not return until I come to you."

"Should Thaddeus not accompany us? He is the king's gu–"

"I need him at the palace. There is no time to explain. Just go." He could not tell her about Alexis. Not yet.

He shoved Melina, turning her towards Trachis. Agrias held his eye a moment longer before nodding his understanding and placing an arm over his wife's shoulder, taking her and Ava away.

Dimly I became aware of a commotion in the room. The soldiers around me charged, but I did not look up from Alexis' pale face. I took in the features I had known and loved for so many winters. Her death would not go unpunished. I would make Ares and his soldiers pay with their lives.

I took a deep breath and set Alexis gently on the floor, pressing my lips to her forehead. "I shall make it right," I whispered.

I stood, my eyes sweeping the room and finding a discarded sword. It was Thaddeus who had arrived, his weapon a blur as he dispatched one of the soldiers. Ares was where I had left him. I grabbed the sword and set my feet in readiness. Ares smirked. He still had the dagger in his hand; Alexis' blood dripped down the blade and covered his fingers.

He pulled out his sword, motioning for me to come at him. Anger replaced the desperate loss inside me, exploding through my blood as I squeezed the handle of my xiphos in my palm. I screamed with anger, with pain, with all that I had, and launched myself at him. Iron met iron with a deafening clang but Ares pushed me away easily.

"Ava shall never know about the amulet," I told him. I may have failed Alexis, but I would not fail our daughter. I would not allow Ares to have her.

"That choice is no longer yours. When her time comes, she shall *want* to know of it. She shall desire a weapon so powerful it can take down all of her enemies with one motion. She shall remember this night as the night the Persians were here. From now on, they shall be her greatest enemy." He took a step towards me, wiping Alexis' blood from the knife onto his cuirass. "Ava shall remember that they took her mothers from her so tragically. She shall grow with a fire inside her and when she sees a Persian soldier, she shall be reminded of what they did to her."

He took another step and I straightened my shoulders, feeling the back of my sandal touch Alexis' arm. I set myself to attack.

"I shall use that knowledge and when she knows of the amulet, she shall do whatever I want. The Persians shall reach Greece's shores one day soon. They have grand plans to extend their influence. They want Athens for themselves ... and I shall help them take it."

"Ava shall never be yours," I promised, my fist clenching. "If my blood does indeed run through her then she shall deny you what you want. She shall defeat you."

Ares laughed. "You wish. Unfortunately it is not something you shall ever see, or have influence over," he shrugged.

Leandros skidded to a halt inside the doorway of the Throne Room. Alexis was on the ground, eyes closed. Thaddeus fought one of Ares' soldiers, another two lay dead nearby. Thaddeus sliced the edge of his sword across the man's throat, though not before another of the soldiers fired an arrow through Thaddeus' back, the tip poking out through his stomach. Leandros disarmed the man with the bow, cutting a deep gash into his thigh, and crashing the pommel of his sword against his temple. Thaddeus fell to his knees, his hands at his stomach.

Leandros' gaze went to his daughter. "Skylar!"

I heard my father's voice and faltered in my intended attack against the God of War. My momentary loss of concentration was all Ares needed. He was at my side in an instant. The sword slipped from my grasp. My heated blood trickled down my throat. Ares stepped away, grinning. I had not even seen him raise the knife to slice me open as he moved towards me. I clutched uselessly at the gaping wound at my neck, my knees finding the hard ground below. I tried to scream, but no sound came out and the more I attempted, the quicker I felt my life draining from me. I wanted to fight, but I had nothing left to give.

"No!" Leandros cried, rushing forward. He barely got three steps before Ares swept him up into the purple circle he so favored.

"Meddlesome mortals," Ares murmured.

Leandros banged uselessly on the rounded edge, able only to watch as his daughter was taken from him, just as his Zita had been so many winters ago, and by the same master.

Ares crouched down and loosened the knotted leather at my neck. "You shall not be in need of this any longer," he said, taking the amulet.

I wanted to reach for it, to deny him, but neither my limbs nor my voice would obey me any longer. I slumped, face first to the marble floor. My vision dimmed as it had when I was stabbed on the plain of the Spercheios Valley when I arrived in the region of Malis. This time Ares would not heal my wounds and I would not wake to the gentle ministrations of Alexis, Princess of Trachis. I would go to her in the Underworld. I would find her there, of that I had no doubt. She would forgive me for not saving her. For not saving myself. We shared a love that would last not only in this world, but in the next, and for as many as we found ourselves in for all time.

As I succumbed to the knowledge that I was done in this life, my thoughts turned to Ava. I prayed that she would be strong enough to resist the God of War if and when the time came; that she could do more to deny him of what he wanted with her. I hoped she could do more than I had been able to for her today. I prayed my father would keep her safe and far from Ares, guiding her to follow a path that did not lead her to join him and his plan for mortals and gods. I prayed that one day, if she needed it, that I could somehow help her from Hades' realm.

Leandros collapsed inside the bubble, sobbing, eyes fixed on his dead daughter.

"Enough, old man. It is done," Ares said. The God of War returned his features to his own before disappearing in his flash of brilliant light, a final, manic laugh torturing Leandros as it echoed around him.

The purple snare vanished and Leandros crawled across to Skylar, lifting her head into his lap. "My beautiful girl ..." he murmured, brushing the hair from her forehead and kissing her gently. He allowed another wail to emerge and beat at his chest until his knuckles bled.

Leandros did not know how long he sat there, howling and holding his child, but he did not stop until Moeris' firm hand gripped his shoulder. Agrias and Ophelos joined them, the king collapsing in his own grief as he found the broken body of Alexis.

Moeris carefully scooped up Skylar as Ophelos aided Leandros to his feet, guiding him around Thaddeus' still body; hands folded across his stomach, eyes wide in his death.

None of Ares' soldiers remained, the only trace of their existence the pools of blood and discarded weapons on the marble floor. Agrias could barely carry Alexis, Brygos taking her from his king, while another of Trachis' soldiers gathered up Thaddeus. The solemn procession left the Throne Room, heading first to the room that had

belonged to Alexis and Skylar.

Though he was beset with grief, Moeris kept his tears at bay, determined to assist his friends and his king with whatever preparations were needed to send his princess, her lover, and Agrias' favored guard to the Underworld. He would always regret he had not arrived sooner to defend them, protect them, and he vowed that they would receive the highest respect and would be remembered and mourned for deeply for all they had done for Trachis. They deserved that from him at least.

22

Leandros had greeted the dawn with a heavy heart and candlemarks of waiting. Ava had been curled up on his chest as they lay beside Nasrin in the house they shared with Ophelos and Aspasia. When his granddaughter woke some time later, she hounded him with questions he could not – or would not – answer. Why had the Persians come? Where were they now? Why did they not remain if they intended to rule Trachis? She had cried and raged in equal measure and he had held her throughout, sharing her pain, though not her confusion at why her mothers had been taken from her.

He stood now just inside the door to Skylar and Alexis' room at the palace, greeting the mourners. Townspeople and family had begun arriving two candlemarks ago, following Leandros' approval of how his daughter was to be dressed for the viewing.

Hesper and the queen had been in charge of the preparations of the bodies the previous day, though if Melina had had her way, Skylar would not have been afforded the same funeral rights as her daughter. It had been Hesper who had convinced the queen to allow it, volunteering for the job herself and ensuring it was carried out properly, and to the standard Skylar deserved. Leandros had been touched by the young woman's care and strength, especially given that she had lost her own beloved husband to the same enemy.

Hesper had washed clean the blood and remnants of death from

Skylar's body and hair and applied oil to her skin before placing a wreath atop her head and dressing Skylar in her tunic and leather cuirass. Her sandals also soon found her feet and her trusted sword laid at her side. She would be set atop her funeral pyre in the same manner, less her sword, the following day and when her body was only ashes, she would be placed in an amphora and taken to her final resting place. The king and Leandros had agreed where that would be alone.

"There is a cluster of laurel trees, near the hot springs. When Alexis was with child, she spoke with me about placing the ashes from her pyre, and of Skylar's when her time came, beneath them, buried deep in the soil in an amphora," King Agrias had said. *"She held concern at that time for herself during the childbirth process, and did not want to be taken to Macedonia where one day I shall be buried. Would you permit Skylar to be put to rest there with Alexis now, or is there somewhere else you would prefer?"*

"The hot springs are fitting, though it should be Ava who is given the task of seeing them interred. She shall need that. And somewhere to visit them," Leandros had replied.

The king had agreed and departed. Where he went Leandros did not ask, and it was of no concern to him. His darling Ava needed him more than anyone else and he would not leave her alone for long with her swirling thoughts.

Ava sat beside Skylar's body, the queen beside Alexis' on the opposite side of the bed, both wrapped in dark himations and chanting out dirges as they wept and pulled at their hair and clothing. Though they were genuinely grieving, the actions of beating at their breasts and pulling at themselves were mostly symbolic gestures, and expected during the formal mourning period known as the prosthesis.

In contrast to their cries and movements, Alexis was still, dressed in a beautiful chiton of royal purple. Just as she had the day Leandros and Skylar first saved her from Melanthios in the Spercheios Valley, she wore a long himation which covered her from head to foot, her hair hidden beneath it and the veil laid carefully up to reveal her face. Whereas that first himation had been in yellow, this one was in purple to match her chiton, and to indicate to those who saw her that she was of the highest royal esteem in Trachis. There would be no mistaking that, and though Leandros wished Skylar bore some semblance of purple to show how esteemed she also was to the town, he knew she would be far more comfortable waking in the Underworld with her armor.

Both girls' mouths were left unsealed, an agreement hard fought, and won, by Leandros against Melinda. He insisted that though it was tradition to seal a coin inside for their journey, that Ava be allowed place them there before the pyres were set alight. Again it had been Hesper who had spoken in favor of the decision and convinced the queen to allow it. She told Melina that she intended for her own children to be allowed do the same for their father when he was sent to Hades; Thaddeus' body having been prepared akin to Skylar and Alexis'. Hesper had returned to their home a candlemark before to greet her own family and friends who wished to pay their respects. Leandros intended to make his way there with Ava when the last of Skylar's mourners left.

23

The ekphora – or funeral procession – gathered before dawn three days after Skylar, Alexis and Thaddeus were killed. Leandros and Moeris carried Skylar's body, Agrias and Ophelos in front with Alexis', and Thaddeus' kin behind with him. They made their way from the palace of Trachis, through the town and agora, to the beach at the edge of the Malian Gulf, more and more followers joining them as they went. The island of Euboea was just an outline in the distance when Eos weakly illuminated the sky with her pink dawn, though few eyes settled on it, drawn instead to the pyres lined up and the flickering torches wedged into the sand around them.

The carriers settled their burdens atop the boughs of olive and laurel trees that Moeris and the soldiers had collected. Sprigs of rosemary had been pushed between the branches to serve as tinder – normally other small twigs would be used, but the smell of sulphur from the hot springs was strong, reaching them there on that particular morning when usually it would not. Perhaps the springs knew they were the next destination of the mourners and wished to lead them safely to their banks. Whatever the reason, Moeris had thought to mention it to the king and Leandros well before anyone else had reached the beach, sending one of the newer ephebes to collect the scented herb and mask the smell somewhat.

The wind was cold as it whipped off the water and Leandros pulled his himation closer. Many other mourners did the same, murmuring quietly as they did so. Only Ava remained without either a himation over her tunic or words to be spoken. The wind lashed at her hair; reminding Leandros how similar she was to Skylar at the same age. Of course if the day's light had been stronger, he knew he would see the most obvious difference – the green of her eyes which matched Alexis'.

Leandros took two torches, lighting them from a third stuck in the ground. The wind threatened to extinguish them again, but Moeris and two other soldiers stepped forward to shield the struggling flames and Leandros handed one to Agrias. He motioned to Ava to join him and she stepped forward slowly. He reached down and lifted her up, watching as she squeezed her eyes shut tight and drew in a deep breath.

"You have the coins?" he asked quietly.

She opened her eyes and nodded, holding them up for him to see. He nodded in reply and took her to Alexis and then Skylar, holding her tightly as she placed her thumb on their chins to open their mouths. After closing each again, she closed her eyes briefly, her lips moving in silent words he could only imagine were prayers.

Leandros would have been content to hold his granddaughter as he prepared to press the head of the torch to Skylar's pyre, but she squirmed in his arms and he set her down on the sand again. At a solemn nod from Agrias, Leandros held the torch out for Ava to place her hand above his and together they set alight the body of her Mumma.

Leandros bent his head and closed his eyes, sending up his own words of comfort and love to his daughter, her lover and their dear friend, Thaddeus. He could not imagine how it would be in Trachis without the three of them, though he knew he must show strength as he lived the rest of his life. Not only for them, but for Ava who would rely on him now to keep their memory alive.

24

Late in the afternoon, once the pyres and the bodies atop them had burnt down to no more than piles of ash, Leandros and Agrias had gathered up what remained of their daughters; Hesper doing the same at Thaddeus' pyre beside them. Hampered by the wind which continued to whip up along the beach, Moeris had attached lengths of cloth to the cold torches to prevent the ashes from being blown away before they could be collected and stored in the amphorae.

As the sun set behind Mount Kallidromon, a small gathering formed at the hot springs to lay Skylar and Alexis to rest for the final time. Though he was not there now, Moeris had dug the holes for the amphorae earlier so Ava could place them inside without difficulty. With torches placed in a circle around the laurel trees Agrias had spoken of, Leandros, Agrias and Melina stood behind Ava, watching on as she sealed the containers and slipped them inside the waiting earth. Hesper and her family had made their own goodbyes to Thaddeus in the same place earlier.

The three adults joined Ava on their knees and Leandros handed her Skylar's dagger. Ava cut two long strands from her hair, returning the weapon to him so he, Agrias and Melina could do the same; all of them placing them on the amphorae when they were done. A mixture of varying amounts honey, water, wine, oil and perfume followed the hair onto the vessels, the familiar scents of both girls swirling in the breeze around the grievers.

When the liquid had been absorbed by the dirt, Leandros laid his hand on Ava's shoulder. She looked up at him, tears staining her face. He picked her up, needing no words of request to wrap his arms around her, nor she to bury her head at his chest as her body shuddered with her sobs. In silence he carried her back to the palace, wishing he could simply take her to her room and ensure she slumbered safely in his arms. But there was the funerary feast to be held in the andron, and both of them were expected to attend, whether it was what they wanted or not.

25

A res watched the woman attempt to convince herself not to go through with her decision, then war and rage the other side of the debate, moving ever closer to the edge of the cliff. Though she could not see the immortal being who stood beside her, the God of War could. After all, Moros was brother to Eris and the Keres, and enjoyed nothing more than assisting Ares with any dark deed he requested.

Moros was known by many names; doom, Ares' favorite. He could drive any man or woman towards their own inevitable destruction – it was why the God of War had chosen him for this particular task in the first place.

Too many people had already offered to take in and care for Ares' Chosen One, and he did not wish for that. He needed her alone, focused, unhampered by family or friends. She must harbor her thoughts of revenge and be prepared to act upon them without worry of recrimination from those closest to her.

The woman – Hesper – was only one of those who stood in his way and what Ares had in mind for her was quite final. For all concerned. Her death would reach the lives of many, would orphan three other children and push his Chosen One aside in the minds of those who stood nearby. Yes, he needed to end this today. Then he would see to the other mortal who needed to be removed from

Ava's side.

"I just cannot bear to go on. Not without him. He was everything to me. How could I love another when he gave me all I ever wanted? Ever needed," Hesper wailed to no one in particular. "But if I am no longer here, who shall take care of my children? Of Ava? She is akin to one of my own. Thaddeus' blood runs through her. She and Eumelia are so close, and on the precipice of being women. How can I leave them now? Without Alexis and Skylar here, who shall teach her of the world she is about to enter?"

Back and forth it went for half-a-candlemark or so, until finally Moros tipped her with a final thought; when I reach the Underworld, I shall see not only Thaddeus again, but Tritonos. My boys shall be waiting for me when I arrive.

And with that, she threw herself from the cliff face, not a shred of fear in her heart. With a smile on her face, she hit the jagged rocks at the bottom, every bone in her body breaking on impact, the waves crashing over and washing the blood from the discolored tips, and her body back to the shore.

Those at the palace of Trachis who participated in the funeral banquet for the princess and Skylar knew nothing of the carnage taking place at the west gate, or the sorrow that would once again grip them with tight hands. They would soon enough. Ares had ensured that Hesper's body would be found by the fishermen returning to Trachis. For now though, there was someone else he needed to rid Trachis of.

26

Leandros watched as Agrias approached, dressed in the bright purple which marked him as royal. Before their daughters' deaths, the king had taken to only wearing the color for official functions, and though the banquet could be considered an official matter, Agrias had barely been without his colors since that night, even when expected to wear the black mourning himation. Not that Leandros could fault him, for he had remained in his armor, weapons at his side, since then also. He slept in the uncomfortable cuirass even when Nasrin begged him to remove it. For some reason he just could not bring himself to do so.

Leandros and Agrias had shared few words since ... it had happened. They had not argued, disagreed, or outright blamed one another for the incident in the Throne Room as Leandros and the queen had, yet there had been little warmth and friendship between them. Both were too lost in their personal grief to find words of comfort for the other.

"Leandros, would you join us in the Throne Room? There are words to be shared," Agrias said, arriving in front of the Thracian.

"Of course," Leandros nodded, lifting the sleeping child from his lap and placing her in Nasrin's instead. Ava stirred, her eyes opening as he removed his arms. He placed a kiss on her forehead. "Remain asleep, my darling, I shall return soon."

She shook her head, stretching and hopping down to stand next to him, slipping her hand into his. "I shall join you. Whatever Grandfather Agrias has to say to you, he can say to me, just as we have always agreed on."

Leandros grinned tightly, kneeling down to her height and squeezing her hand. "It appears you were not sleeping as deeply as I suspected." The girl shrugged but returned his smile. Leandros looked up to Agrias, his eyebrows raised in question.

The king gave a faint shake of his head. "Not this time. Please, Ava." His words came out choked and Leandros wondered what caused such a reaction. The two men had shared many conversations that their granddaughter had insisted on being part of – some they would never have imagined she would be privy to. But never had Agrias so utterly pleaded with her to leave them to their words.

Leandros gripped Ava's hand again, his eyes returning to hers. "Remain with Nasrin, I shall return soon and then I believe it is time you found yourself meeting Hypnos."

Ava appeared to sense, just as he had, that the king's request was not usual and she hesitated only a moment before nodding and returning to Nasrin's arms. She was an observant child and Leandros wondered if she had been witness to the arguments he and Melina had had since her mothers were killed.

Leandros followed Agrias to the Throne Room, the two of them stopped only twice by those who had joined them for the funeral banquet in the andron. Melina awaited them on her throne, her face set in one recently familiar to Leandros – partway between grief and anger as she stared him down.

He stood before them, his eyes straying to the place where, until so recently, Skylar's blood had stained the marble. He wished their conversation could take place anywhere but in that room. He wanted to ask how Agrias and Melina could possibly want to conduct any business there, but until he was given the opportunity to speak freely with Agrias, he would not utter a word. Briefly, he wondered if they felt closer to Alexis there, he had certainly heard of such attachments being formed. For him though, it was not the case and he hoped their words did not cause him to linger there for long.

"Leandros, answer me," Melina ordered, bringing Leandros from his musing.

"Apologies," he muttered, wishing once more to be down at the Melas River, fishing with Ava or training with the men, hearing Skylar's commands and directions as she taught the young ephebes. "What was your question?"

"I asked you where the amulet is."

"I do not know."

"You must have some idea."

"I do not."

"Think," she insisted.

Leandros frowned. He had no idea and he did not care. It was the least of what he cared about, and it was not the first time he had told her so.

"It is gone Melina, it disappeared when Skylar was ... when she ... It is just gone," he finally managed, his voice low.

"Could Ava have taken it?" Melina continued.

"No, she was nowhere near them ... afterwards. You know that."

"But if she did?" she hounded.

He blew out a deep breath, his anger stirring. "She does not carry Skylar's mark, it is of no consequence."

"How can we be certain? We have been beset by problem after problem since you and your daughter arrived. If you had not come here, then our daughter would still be alive."

"How quickly you appear to forget it was *you* who pushed our children together more than anyone else. You did not wish for Alexis to return to Epirus," Leandros countered.

"Melina, please, if Leandros and Skylar had not come, we would have been enslaved to the Illyrians or the Persians many winters ago," Agrias entered the conversation, the voice of reason.

"The Persians were only here because of them," Melina cried, ignoring his remark about the Illyrians.

Unseen by anyone in the room, Ares took his chance, grinning as he leant close to the queen and murmured words she would always believe she had thought of.

"He cannot stay any longer. Leandros, I hereby banish you from the city of Trachis in the region of Malis, land of the Malians, and the greater region of Thermopylae. You are not to return. Ever."

"I understand," Leandros finally replied in a quiet voice.

"No Papou! Do not leave. You cannot leave," Ava cried, bursting into the room. *Gods, how long has she been there, listening? Hearing us argue?* Leandros wondered.

His granddaughter clung desperately to his thigh, her tears staining his leather armor as she sobbed. Leandros removed her hands from his legs, kneeling down so their heads were level. He wrapped his arms around her, his heart breaking as her body convulsed with shuddering breath and fresh tears. Another loss for her to endure. Their separation was inevitable, but he knew there was so much he should tell her.

Perhaps he would return for her; steal her away under a cover of darkness. She had Philo, they could be in Sparta by week's end. Perhaps it was time he made himself known to Leonidas. Perhaps there he and Ava would find a new family to be part of. Melina would not be able to take Ava back if the Spartan army stood to protect her. A flicker of satisfaction flared at that thought, as another just as quickly took its place; at least Skylar had known of her brother before she died. There were no secrets between them any longer. He placed his mouth at Ava's ear.

"My darling, I must. When it is time, I shall come find you and tell you everything. I give you my word," he whispered. Leandros leaned back ever so slightly, finding Ava's eyes with his own as Moeris took her from his grasp.

She struggled against the soldier, grabbing for her grandfather, but Leandros did not reach for her – allowing Moeris to take her. He did not resist as he too was hauled to his feet and dragged away.

"Swear you shall find me?" she screamed.

"I shall find you. I love you my darling and we shall see each other again," Leandros promised. He smiled at his beloved granddaughter, hoping it was not long before he laid eyes on her again, and praying to any god who would listen that they take care of her until they were reunited.

He walked backwards slowly, never breaking the gaze that held his in return, the soldiers no longer dragging, but rather guiding him, from the room when they realized he would make no attempt to fight them. *I hope I never have to tell you anything about Ares*, he thought as they cleared the doorway and Ava's face was lost to him.

27

"Where shall we go?" Nasrin asked, her voice quiet.

Leandros hesitated, still attempting find the answer himself. There was one place he knew they must visit before they decided on any other. Initially, he had intended to remain close enough to Trachis that he could return and take Ava as well away but, as if sensing his intentions, Melina had seen to it that he and Nasrin were escorted over the mountains and far away from the town sooner rather than later.

His farewell with the king had been fond enough, and warmer certainly than it had been between them for days; the ruler allowing him and Nasrin until the following morning to gather what they wanted to take and make their goodbyes.

"You cannot convince the queen to change her mind?" Nasrin had asked Agrias. "You shall not speak to her and convince her that sending Leandros away from Ava is not the right decision?"

"I have attempted to persuade her, but this ... she ... I have never seen her so determined before. It may take some time. But know that I will speak on your behalf when I feel the time is appropriate," the king had replied, taking first Nasrin, then Leandros' hands in his own two and squeezing gently. *"I shall miss you, my friends."*

"And we you," Leandros had replied with a nod. There was a pause, then the two grasped each other in a tight hug, needing no words to communicate the deep loss each felt for their children, and

their ending friendship.

When they saw the distant village of Amphissa – where so long ago Leandros had purchased Skaris – Moeris, with a heavy heart and yet another apology, released Leandros and Nasrin from the ropes that held them and allowed them to mount Skotos and Raisa and be on their way. Leandros had been forced to leave much behind, but he vowed that Skylar's horse would not be one of them. He spoke at length with Agrias of his reasons for wanting to take Skotos, though his friend did not need lengthy explanation to grant his wish. He would have given Leandros anything he asked for. Except Ava.

Leandros had queried Agrias in a round-about way as to her future and had been told that she was to remain, that Agrias would do whatever he had to, to ensure her safety, including standing against Leandros. Trachis was her home, he told Leandros, and she would be expected to take Agrias' place as leader one day. She needed to learn what it was to be in charge of those people. Her people.

Though it crushed him to allow it, Leandros knew Agrias spoke true, and he attempted to put aside the thoughts of taking her from where she belonged. He hoped Philo and the murex shell Skylar had given her for her birthing day celebration so recently would be enough physical reminders of her mothers, along with Alexis' parents and kin. What she kept inside would be far more precious, though with his banishment, he could not influence how much or how little she recalled of her mothers, or the parts of them she mirrored. That too would be decided by Agrias and Melinda.

"Sparta," Leandros finally replied, lifting his gaze from the path ahead of them to meet Nasrin's.

"Oh?" she asked, her tone and face showing her curiosity.

He nodded, thankful once again that Nasrin had had no hesitation in declaring her intention to join him when she got word of what the queen had demanded of him.

"Cleomenes should not hear of Skylar's demise from anyone other than me. I shall advise him to cut ties with Trachis."

"You wish to turn him against Agrias?"

"No."

"But you believe the Spartan King shall sever his alliance with Trachis because Skylar is ... no longer in this world?" she asked.

"He was only bound to *her*, to what she had asked him so she could betroth Alexis. I do not believe he would see his allegiance remain to Trachis if she is not in it."

Nasrin nodded, and Leandros saw her considering her words. "Are we to remain with him there after you deliver such news? Shall you finally speak of your kinship with Leonidas?"

Leandros blew out a deep breath. "I have given the matter consideration, but Sparta is not where we are needed. When I have spoken with Cleomenes, we shall travel to Persia and assist our men and whoever else Aristagoras was able to convince to join him in his cause against Darius."

Nasrin watched him a long moment, her gaze never wavering as she spoke again. "You are certain that is a battle you wish to immerse yourself in? Skylar did not want us there."

"Skylar has no say in this decision," Leandros replied angrily.

"I understand that," Nasrin acknowledged with a slight nod of her head, softening her tone. "I only want to ensure you are not deciding to go there because she so vehemently opposed it. You are angry with her for leaving you. For leaving Ava. Though you have not, and would never, speak those particular words, I see it is the truth." Leandros opened his mouth to speak, but Nasrin reached out and squeezed him arm, keeping him silent. "You are heartbroken and angry at having to leave; torn by your desire to run far from the town that caused you so much pain, and wanting to remain close to watch Ava grow. I understand it. I grieve with you. For you. For all of us."

Leandros exhaled another deep breath, recalling the sadness with which he had snuck away earlier that morning under Moeris' watchful gaze and Nasrin's tight grip, long before Eos' dawn crept over the city. It was his decision, his plan, so he would not have to say goodbye to Ava again, nor she to him. Neither of them could have beared it, he was certain of that.

"I shall not show you disrespect by denying what you say. And perhaps I am using the opportunity to travel across the waters to Persia as an excuse to get away from Trachis, and to turn my back on what my daughter wanted. But we could be of use in Persia. And I need to be useful. I have nothing to offer Greece by remaining here. But there ... there I can do what I could not here. I know you understand that also." Nasrin only nodded in reply. "As dearly as I wish to have Ava with us, she cannot travel where we are to go. She does not need to be exposed to the certain carnage and death we shall see. Kleitos, Sander, Hektor and Demosthenes are there and I shall not allow them to die at the hands of Darius. I must ensure they return to Trachis and Sparta and have the opportunity to find wives or lovers and enjoy them well into old age. I *have* to do this."

"Then we shall go to Sparta. And then to Persia," Nasrin said, slipping her fingers between Leandros'. "Perhaps some time away may see heated words cool and hearts open once again to friends."

"Perhaps," Leandros agreed, bringing Nasrin's hand to his lips, though he could not imagine Melina changing her mind. And he did not know how he could ever begin to forgive her for her words and actions either.

28
12ᵗʰ moon full, Moon of Mounichion, 498BC

Leandros pulled strongly on the oar he had been assigned. Nasrin sat in front of him, her arms straining with her own efforts. The bireme travelled swiftly over the calm waters, taking them ever closer to Ephesus, where they would meet up with the Ionians and begin their march towards Sardis to face the Persians, the true enemies of Nasrin, and the assumed enemies of Ava.

With little else to think of as they travelled, Leandros' thoughts drifted over what the past winter had held for he and Nasrin. Much had changed, and though he and his lover had spoken of travelling to Persia, it had taken them almost fourteen more moons to see that decision realized.

From where Moeris had left them at Amphissa, Leandros and Nasrin had travelled to Sparta, reaching the unfamiliar, yet well-known city, in a little over a week. Their time there was longer than Leandros had originally intended – remaining for an entire moon all told. He and Cleomenes spoke of much, though Leandros kept knowledge of Leonidas' entwined kinship to himself.

Cleomenes comforted Leandros and Nasrin in their tears, shedding many of his own for his lost friend. He took the two of them to Rachi, just as he had Skylar, and mourned for her as if she had been a Spartan king; telling the inhabitants of the small village of her death as he beat a cauldron. He then insisted that a man and woman from every home join him, striking at their foreheads with lament. For the next ten days, not one of them worked on producing the purple dye or procuring the murex shells they were known for, as a mark of respect for their king's lost friend.

From Rachi, they returned to Sparta, where Cleomenes dissolved the partnership he and Skylar had formed, sending a messenger to Agrias to convey his sadness at Skylar and Alexis' passing and to offer his sympathies. The messenger also carried word of Cleomenes' decision to break the alliance. Leandros did not know how Agrias would react to the news, and so when Cleomenes requested it of him, he remained in Sparta to hear Agrias' decision. Neither Cleomenes nor Leandros wanted to become Agrias' enemy, and were relieved when Agrias accepted the Spartan king's decision and kind offer that should Trachis ever need Spartan assistance, he would only need to ask it.

While they waited for Agrias' return message, Leandros had asked Cleomenes to find out where Aristagoras had gone after Sparta, and how the rebellion against Darius was going. After a time, they learned that Athens had agreed to send twenty triremes from their fleet to assist, though they waited for the Eretrians in Euboea to build the five biremes they had pledged to Aristagoras before sailing east. Leandros made the decision to go to Athens and assist them in crafting new armor for the soldiers they would send with the boats, and they departed Sparta soon after Agrias' reply arrived.

Leandros and Nasrin remained in Athens for six moons before going to Eretria and helping to build the biremes, hoping their assistance could hasten the progress being made on the island. Given that the closest harbor was Delphinium, Nasrin suggested they leave Skotos and Raisa with Archippos as they had when they travelled to Naxos two winters' before.

Leandros had dismounted from Skotos, the front door of the house opening and a curious head popping out.

"Skotos!" came the excited reply, the door flung wide to spit out the racing child.

For just a moment, Leandros' chest tightened – the boy so close in age to Ava. He swallowed and felt for Nasrin's hand. She was instantly beside him, needing no words to sense his need for her and squeezing him tightly when their palms collided.

With the horses taken care of in Delphinium, Leandros and Nasrin boarded the small boat and sailed the two candlemarks across the Gulf of Euboea to Eretria, beginning work immediately and tirelessly on the ships with the other craftsmen who were on the island for the same purpose.

The two of them would have remained there until the task was complete, had the first anniversary of Skylar, Alexis, Thaddeus and Hesper's deaths not arrived. Though she wished to make the journey with Leandros, Nasrin chose to remain on the island, working without complaint or danger while Leandros made the journey back to Trachis alone.

He left with the new moon of Anthesterion, collecting Skotos from Archippos and arriving in Trachis four days later. He had kept in contact with Moeris, and it was the commander of the army who met him at the laurel trees at the hot springs. The following evening – exactly a winter to the day since their children had died – Agrias and Melina arrived at the hot springs, making their offerings of food at the amphorae as was custom. Ava was not with them but Leandros was not surprised to find it so. Moeris had told him of the rift which had opened up between the three of them since his banishment and so he remained out of sight until they were gone and Ava arrived.

Leandros wanted to appear to her. He knew it was dangerous – that her wish to join him would be even more heightened than it had been a winter ago – and he knew he was not prepared to take her to Persia. Still, he wanted her to know that he still thought of her every day, and wanted to hear if she did of him as well. He dropped silently from the tree he sat watching in, intending to do just that, when Agrias' hand found his shoulder and he commanded the man's silence and immobility.

Leandros was so surprised to see the king, the friend, he had so fiercely missed the past winter that he remained where he was. By the time he recovered himself, Ava had left again.

"I knew you would return this night," the king had said.

"How could I not?" Leandros replied.

"I have missed you," Agrias murmured, taking him in a crushing embrace.

"And I you," Leandros managed, squeezing the smaller man in return.

They had spoken for a number of candlemarks, Moeris joining them and offering to travel some of the way back to Delphinium with Leandros when he was ready to leave again.

"Where does Melina believe you are?" Leandros could not help himself from asking.

"She knows where I am. She too believed you would come this night. Though she is of the thought that I shall deny you your right to mourn and send prayers to your daughter where she lays now. But I would never do so."

"And for that I am grateful."

"I would deny no father the same opportunity. If Melina's heart was not so broken, I am certain she would allow the same."

"So she has not softened towards me or my return then?"

"I am sorry to say, but no."

Leandros nodded, believing Moeris would have spoken of it already if it was so. "And Ava? Where is she?"

"Not where her grandmother believes she is," Moeris replied with a tight grin.

"Oh, and where is that?"

"Ava has recently left the palace. She remains with Ophelos and Aspasia. The room you once occupied with Nasrin is now hers," Agrias answered.

"All is not well between you," Leandros said, a statement, not a question.

"It has been … difficult since you left," Agrias nodded.

"But she is well, within herself?" Leandros pressed.

The king shrugged. *"I cannot say for certain for she does not speak with me. She blames me for your departure and how can I refute her words when she speaks with truth?"*

Leandros nodded, placing his hand on his friend's shoulder, none of them speaking for a long moment.

"You said she is not where Melina believes her to be – with Ophelos and Aspasia. Is she with Eumelia and her brothers instead?" Leandros eventually asked, addressing the commander.

"No. She came to me at the barracks after she was here. I allowed her to attempt sleep there. I understand she feels a connection with Skylar when she is at the barracks and on this day I could not – would not – deny her of any comfort she requires."

Leandros nodded, his thoughts drifting back to that

*fateful night and an ending he still mourned and raged
over in equal measure. "May I ... may I see her?" he
asked quietly.*

"Of course," Moeris replied immediately.

*"I do not believe it wise," Agrias said at the same
time. "I prevented you from speaking with her here
because she is still grieving. Seeing you again would
only hurt her deeper. You cannot take her with you."*

*"I know that and where I am to go I would not
want her to be. But I need to see her."*

*"She shall be asleep," Moeris countered. "She shall
not even know he is here."*

*Agrias hesitated a long moment, but eventually
nodded once.*

His granddaughter had indeed been sleeping when he snuck into the
barracks and Moeris' simple quarters. He had stroked her hair and
kissed her forehead, whispering words of love and hope for her
before straightening. He hoped Morpheus was kind to her if ever she
found herself in his realm, though if she was akin to Leandros, it
would not be so and he allowed the silent tears to fall as he watched
the rise and fall of her shoulders.

Leandros spoke little of what he had learned in Trachis when he
returned to Nasrin in Eretria. Instead, he worked himself even harder
on the final boat. Having never assisted in the creation of a vessel
before, he paid close attention to how it was brought together,
learning that the Eretrians worked from the outside in. First the hull
was created, and it began as a pure warship with fifty oars of twenty-
five per side; the Eretrians called it a penteconter. At almost one
hundred and twenty-five feet long and thirteen feet wide it had a top
speed of nine and a half knots and a deadly bronze prow which was
suitable for ramming enemy ships should they need to.

A triangular frame was then added to the penteconter which
allowed for a second level of oars to be fitted, making it a bireme
with one hundred rowers rather than only fifty. The ship builders told
Leandros that the speed of the vessel would be somewhat reduced,
but it allowed them to take more soldiers to Persia to ensure victory.

With two levels of rowers, the lower men sat towards the center
of the ship with the oars fixed on the hull, whilst the ones on the
upper bench sat towards the outside of the ship, and their oars were
fixed on the additional framework. The boat had only one large,

square sail made of linen cloth and once it was erected, the benches for the rowers and the deck were added.

When the announcement was made that the boats were ready, Leandros was relieved beyond measure that finally they could begin their travel east.

29
Aegean Sea

Loud voices and shouts of excitement grew from the men on the deck above. Leandros and Nasrin were on the bottom level of the two sets of rowers, and as such they could see nothing but the other men around them and the ship's sturdy wooden planks. Even so, word quickly reached them that they would arrive at Coresus in the territory of Ephesus in less than half-a-candlemark at their current pace.

Whilst Leandros and Nasrin were building the biremes at Eretria, Aristagoras had changed the original plans. When the Greeks had first agreed to aid him, the idea was for all the allies to meet in Miletus, where they would combine their forces and leave from. However, Darius' brother, Artaphernes, who still harbored the large debt and much ill-feeling toward Aristagoras, somehow learned of the Milesian's plans of attack and incited his own. He wanted to defeat the rebellion before it had the chance to take hold, and gain back some respect from his brother.

Artaphernes began to march towards Miletus, which left his home of Sardis, the capital of the satrapy of Lydia, and an important stronghold to the Persians, vulnerable. The decision could not have assisted Aristagoras better had he thought of it himself, and he sent word to the Greeks to sail directly to Ephesus where a local man would guide them towards Sardis. He believed they would claim an easy, yet significant, victory.

Aristagoras intended to keep Artaphernes and his men fighting as long as possible far from their home to give the Greeks the best chance at winning, though from what Leandros heard from the men on the deck above, Artaphernes had not joined his soldiers at Miletus, but remained with a small number of his best men in Sardis.

The bireme slid onto the beach at Coresus. Hastily grabbing their weapons, the men united on the sand, regaining their strength after the long days of rowing and ensuring their stomachs were full. When the guide Aristagoras had promised arrived half a day later, along with men from Miletus, they began their march towards the capital. Leandros and Nasrin welcomed four familiar faces as they walked; Demosthenes, Hektor, Sander and Kleitos.

"It is a joy to see you again," Demosthenes said, hugging Leandros tightly.

"And you. We did not receive word of your progress and did not know what to think. I am glad to find you all well."

"You did not?" Hektor asked with a frown. "We sent a messenger as soon as Aristagoras returned with word the Athenians had agreed to assist him. It must have been ... two moons after we first left Trachis."

"Two or three, I would be certain of it," Sander nodded.

"Oh. I have not been in Trachis for over a winter."

"Why not? What battles have seen you travel from our home for so long? What orders have Moeris and Skylar given to our men?"

"Skylar has ..." Leandros faltered.

Nasrin slipped her hand into his and finished his sentence. "Skylar and Alexis no longer walk in this world. Neither does Thaddeus."

"Or Hesper," Leandros added.

"What? What happened?" Hektor asked, pausing. The six of them stepped aside, allowing the soldiers around them to continue along the path.

"They were hunted by an old enemy of mine and when he found them he ... he killed them. I was captured by his men and did not get free quick enough to save them," Leandros replied quietly, his eyes finding his sandals as he spoke. "Hesper felt she could not live without her husband, and joined him in the Underworld mere days later."

He knew they would have more questions but he could not answer them. Not yet. Perhaps not ever. They did not need to know it had been Ares who had killed them. Rather, he would allow them to believe it was Persian soldiers, as most others in Trachis did. Everything else he had said was true enough and it would do for now.

"You have been hunting those enemies ever since – to avenge your kin and friends?" Demosthenes asked, resting his hand lightly on Leandros' back.

"No. I simply could not remain. Nasrin and I decided we must assist in *this* battle against the Persians instead. We have been aiding the Athenians and Eretrians in preparing armor and boats."

"And Ava, has she been with you? Is she here?" Kleitos asked, searching the faces of those around them.

"No. She remains in Trachis. It is best is she remains there."

"She shall sit on the throne when King Agrias and Queen Melina no longer do so," Kleitos stated.

"Yes," Leandros replied simply.

"Then perhaps we should return home. Our experience shall be required there should your enemy return for her as well," the young man continued.

"You do not wish to strike against the Persians when you are so close?" Nasrin asked.

"I do, but perhaps it is not where we should be. Perhaps if we had been in Trachis, this enemy of Leandros' would not have succeeded against our friends and the princess."

"There was nothing you could have done," Leandros assured him. "We are all here now. Tell us what you have learnt of the enemy so we can ensure victory can be had in this place."

Kleitos did not speak again for a long moment, clearly warring with himself as to which direction he should go. Finally he nodded and the five men and Nasrin re-joined the soldiers walking towards Sardis.

The march to Sardis was uneventful and they saw no one on the path their guide had chosen. The man told them that if Artaphernes had learned of their impending arrival, he would be expecting them to come ashore near the Hermus Valley and make their way towards him via Phocea and Sipylum. It was a well-known communication and trade route, which is exactly why the guide had decided to take them the shorter, and more mountainous route, through the town of Hypaepa on the southern slope of Mount Tmolus, and over the mountain itself. He acknowledged that though the path was shorter in distance, it was more difficult to traverse, but it would give the

Greeks the element of surprise to arrive from the south rather than the north-west, and the walled fortification on that side was weaker and less guarded.

And so it was that three days after landing at Coreseus, Leandros, Nasrin and the Greek forces arrived and gained access almost unopposed to the city of Sardis.

Leandros drew Skylar's sword from his side and cut down the Persian soldier facing him. The battle raged around them, Artaphernes' soldiers attempting to get their Satrap to the safety of the acropolis in the higher section of the city, whilst still defending the main city on the lower level. They were fighting a losing battle though given the speed and stealth with which the rebels had entered, caught totally unawares, having not discovered the ships docked at Coreseus, nor any sign of approaching boats from their north. Soldiers from both sides soon littered the streets, their blood darkening the dusty laneways between houses and stalls.

Nasrin remained at Leandros' side, her face set in grim determination as she sent enemies to Hades in the Underworld without hesitation. Her sword and shield worked in unison, defending and attacking with frightening accuracy and Leandros almost lost his own weapon to a new attacker as he watched Nasrin's ferocity with pride. Turning to the man before him, he brought his shield up to defend another advance and the two of them fought fiercely for almost half-a-candlemark, neither able to gain an advantage over the other.

Eventually, Leandros managed to disarm the man, striking his shield against his unprotected side and sending him sprawling to the ground. Replacing the sword, he slid his javelin from his back, running it through the Persian's chest and pinning him in place on the ground, his breath coming in pants as he sought to regain his breath after the epic battle.

The smell of burning flesh and straw and wood reached Leandros' nostrils and they flared in response. He drew his gaze from the dead man at his feet to find most of the buildings around him engulfed by flames.

"Leandros!" Nasrin's terrified scream spun him in place. A Persian soldier had her by the arm and was dragging her from one of the burning buildings. Her weapons were gone, armor hanging from one shoulder and tunic ripped and singed.

Without conscious thought, Leandros retrieved his javelin from the soldier and raced after his lover. She fought the man who held her, but his grip was tight and she could not get free. He saw Leandros approaching, but had no time to draw his weapon before Leandros drove his spear through his stomach and out the other side. Nasrin fell to her knees when he released her, Leandros immediately helping her to her feet and checking her over as he supported her.

"What did he do to you?" he asked, fingering the torn material at her thighs.

"Nothing. Though I have no doubt of his intentions once h–" Nasrin's words were cut short by an arrow which grazed Leandros' arm and lodged in her neck.

"Nasrin! No!" he cried, his hands tightening around her waist as she went limp in his arms. "No, Nasrin, please." Another arrow flew past Leandros' head and he placed Nasrin on the ground, drawing Skylar's sword again and running towards the Persian.

He deflected the barrage of arrows the man sent towards him and crashed against the bow in his hand with all the force he could muster against the inside of his shield. Leandros landed on top of the soldier, driving his sword into his stomach and chest as the bow fell from the man's hand. When Leandros was satisfied he would never rise again, he limped back to Nasrin's slumped form. He threw aside his shield and held her tenderly, tears streaming from his eyes.

Nasrin spoke no words, her life already taken by the arrow's penetrating tip. Her eyes remained open and Leandros closed them, just as he had done with Skylar's in Trachis. He pressed his lips to her forehead, rocking her in his arms as he wept.

"The Persians took your life, just as they always intended. As you always told me they would. I promised you it would not be so, and yet once again I have been unable to keep my word to keep someone I love safe. I have failed you too, Nasrin. I am sorry. I am sorry."

Leandros repeated the words until his voice was hoarse and shouts drew his attention once more. A figure arrived at his side and through his tears, he saw Kleitos beside him, face caked with blood and sweat. His eyes found Nasrin's pale face briefly, before returning to Leandros'.

"I am sorry," he whispered. Leandros only nodded in reply, wiping his cheeks with his arm. "Come, the city is in ruins. Most of the buildings are on fire. There is no coin or spoils of victory to be had here. Aristagoras has the outcome he wanted. Hektor, Demosthenes, Sander and myself have lent our talents to the Ionians for long enough. It is time we returned to Greece. To Trachis. You must return with us and see your Nasrin to the Underworld correctly. I wish to see my mother and father, and my brother, Lysistratos. He caused me annoyance so often, yet I have missed him very much. He and Thaddeus and Hesper's son, Nikomachos, were always close. Both of them shall need my guidance and support now more than ever. As shall Nikomachos' brother Pamphilos."

Leandros wanted to speak to the younger man of his banishment from Trachis but did not have the chance as the other men Kleitos had spoken of arrived. They shared quick words of sorrow for Leandros' loss before Sander made his report.

"The acropolis is on fire. The Persians are forming a defense at the banks of the river in the main square. Are we still to leave this place or shall we stand and fight?"

"I believe we should leave," Kleitos replied. Demosthenes nodded his agreement.

"Persia has taken too much today," Hektor agreed, inclining his head in Nasrin's direction. "I do not want to give them the satisfaction of my body as well."

Leandros wanted to speak words of revenge, of anger, but he had nothing left. He was empty. Lost. Grieving again. He remained silent.

"Then it is decided," Sander announced. "We have a boat in Miletus. We should travel there and leave immediately. Aristagoras shall be too busy with his battle against the Persians to notice we have gone."

Kleitos offered his hand to Leandros and the older man took it, allowing himself to be pulled to his feet, his grip on Nasrin tightening. They left the way they had come – through the fallen wall on the south side of the city, Demosthenes pushing them on quickly as renewed sounds of battle reached them. They were headed towards Mount Tmolus before any Greek or Persian was wise to their departure, or cared that it was so.

*

Harbor of Miletus

"Are you certain you shall not join us in victorious return to Trachis?" Kleitos asked.

"Yes," Leandros replied. "I must go to Babylon."

"Babylon? What is there for you?"

"It is not for me that I travel there, but for Nasrin," he said, his eyes straying to the covered figure he spoke of on the pallet beside them. "It is where she was born and it is where she should be returned to in her death."

"I am certain she would want to be placed wherever you believe she should be," Demosthenes said, offering his arm to Leandros. Leandros took it and they squeezed one another firmly.

In truth, Leandros did not know if it was what Nasrin wanted, but the thought of having to take her back to Greece, to lay her beside her daughter in Konitsa or attempt to lay her with Skylar and Alexis – he just did not have the strength to do so. And besides, her parents were in Babylon and the children she had lost to her first husband. Her other sons, if they were still alive, were also in Persia and they may know of the common tale of her death there. She would want to watch over them from close by.

Demosthenes released Leandros and stepped aboard the boat, his path lit by torches on either side. Hektor approached Leandros next and they gripped one another briefly before he joined the Spartan on the water. The two of them would return to Sparta, though they intended to join Sander and Kleitos at Trachis to offer their condolences to the king and queen within a few moons. When the youngest two approached Leandros, they were not so reserved, hugging the larger man and insisting that he not be too long in returning to Trachis. Again he considered telling them of his banishment, but again he kept the words to himself. They would learn of it soon enough.

"When you return to Trachis, do not speak of seeing me here," he told them. "Not to Ava. Not to anyone. Do not tell her of Nasrin's death either. She has known so much death already. She does not need to learn of more."

"Are you certain? Would she not wish to know you are alive and well?" Kleitos asked.

"Of course, but if she learns that Nasrin is dead, she shall know that I am alone. She shall want to come find me. She is just a child and it would not be safe for her to do so."

"I understand," Kleitos nodded. "You have always been close with her so I imagine your words are true."

"We shall not speak of it, though we shall join her in her joy when you return," Sander added.

"Look in on her when you can, though I know you have other duties at the barracks," Leandros said.

"Of course," they agreed.

With a final wave, Sander and Kleitos joined Hektor and Demosthenes on the small boat, pushing off from the beach and sailing back towards the place Leandros had, for a time, called home.

30

West gate, Pass of Thermopylae
6th moon waning, Mounichion

The God of War did not miss the slight shiver that gripped his Chosen One as he arrived beside her. He grinned but did not reveal himself. Ava sat on the broken wall the Phocians had once built, watching the crashing waves far below. She knew it was where Hesper had spent her final moments but that was not the reason she had gone there; it was because she knew no one would think to look for her there. It was also because it was where her Mumma had often gone when she was troubled – which she only knew because the unseen immortal beside her had told her in her dreams.

The sound of low voices caught her attention and she turned to find Kleitos and Sander, two soldiers who had been gone from Trachis for over a winter, coming along the path. She raised a hand in greeting and jumped down, awaiting their arrival. They hastened towards her, Kleitos reaching her first and lifting her up in a warm embrace.

When he returned her to her feet, his eyes shone with tears. "I am so sorry to hear of your mothers' deaths. I wish I could have been here to aid in defending them."

Ava lifted her chin and the God of War saw the determination gleaming in her bright green eyes and in the set of her shoulders. He knew she had worked hard to ensure she no longer woke in tears or cried out for her mothers. She no longer sought comfort from anyone when she thought of them or when they were mentioned. She would not allow the boy's words to affect her in any way – her reply to him proving it.

"You obviously had another important task to attend."

"Even s–" Kleitos began.

"Where did you go?"

"Persia," Sander replied, reaching out awkwardly to embrace her.

Ares saw her stiffen but her voice was even when she spoke.

"Did you battle the Persian soldiers?"

"Yes," he replied.

"And were you victorious?"

"Yes," Sander said again. "We burnt Sardis to the ground. Darius shall feel the loss of the capital of Lydia from his palace."

"Good," Ava said, a feral grin spreading across her face. Kleitos frowned, but Ava did not give him a chance to say more. "So, you have returned for good?"

"Yes," he nodded.

"Your family shall be pleased." She practically dismissed the two of them with a nod of her head and climbed back onto the wall, a grin still touching the corners of her lips.

Kleitos began to move off down the path, but Sander lingered, looking up at the small girl as he spoke again. "You do not have to fear that any harm shall come to you. Now that we have returned, we shall protect you, even if the Persians come. As soldiers of Thermopylae, we shall protect you – as our princess, and when you are our queen." He nodded curtly and turned on his heel, jogging to catch up to his companion.

"I shall be a soldier, not your queen," Ava murmured, watching him leave.

The God of War grinned as he heard the words. She had begun to find the fire within herself. He could feel it pulsing through her blood. The amulet could sense the change as well, it lit up warmly beneath his leather cuirass and he took it out, holding it close to the girl. It brightened considerably. She scratched at her shoulder blades, her brow creasing as she felt the small bumps that had begun to grow the past few moons. Ares' smile widened. It truly had begun.

"It recognizes her," a voice said beside him. Ares nodded, not needing to face his companion to know old Rizpah had joined him on the crumbling wall.

Rizpah was the sole remaining member of the Chosen One's line, apart from Ava of course. When Ava was born, Rizpah was at the palace, Ares having sent her home before Skylar could end her life as well. She had attempted to take part in the ritual of bringing the child into the world, but her powers were so weak due to her age that Ares had removed her from the circle early on. It was possibly that action alone, and that Skylar did not know who she was, that saved her life.

He had not known then if Rizpah would ever travel again, believing her life was almost at an end, yet here she was, her voice surprisingly strong. He grinned, wondering if it was the renewed prestige the remaining Keres showered upon her for her heritage that had bolstered her again. She had lived with the shame and outright hostility of what Zita had done for so long, hiding herself away at the lake at Stymphalos for all but the most important activities of her kin.

For all the previous children born to the line and all the disappointments they had suffered when they and their daughters turned out *not* to be who Ares waited for, this time there was no doubt that the child in Trachis was the Chosen One. They all knew it. They all felt it. The changes had begun in her – sooner than they had in her mother – more akin to full-blooded Keres who had come before her.

"It does," Ares nodded.

As she had the first time her fingers had swept across the small nodes, Ava pulled at her tunic, attempting to see the skin at her back. She could not lay eyes on them from such an angle – the mirror in her room the best assistance she could hope for, being that she would not speak of them with anyone.

"We should take her with us now. We need to begin teaching her to use the amulet, and of her heritage. There is nothing to keep her here and she is not happy. With us, she would never feel that way," Rizpah said.

"No. She remains here until it is time."

"Does the amulet's reaction not tell you that the time is now? You see the bumps beneath her skin – her wings threaten to emerge."

"It is not time," Ares insisted. "Find a way to suppress them."

"We should use her *now*. She is powerful and we need to harness that power."

"Her power comes, but she is not ready. She is but a child, she knows nothing of the world outside Trachis. I shall craft a warrior. My warrior. I shall craft my Chosen One into the soldier I need her to be."

"And how long must we wait for you to do that?" Rizpah questioned boldly.

Ares turned slowly, his gaze piercing through her, his jaw clenched in rage. "You wish to question me?" he asked, his fury barely held at bay.

"Of course not, but …"

"But nothing. When I decide it is time, I shall announce it and not before. Until then, I shall guide her in my own way and if you do not wish to find yourself with the rest of your family, you shall obey me."

Rizpah dropped her eyes from his and nodded. "Apologies, Master. I meant no disrespect. After so many winters, my excitement that she has finally arrived simply overtook me momentarily and I spoke out of turn. I shall leave you to craft your warrior and wait for further orders."

"Good," Ares growled. "Now ensure her wings remain beneath her skin until I come for you again, unless you feel your power is too weak to do even that."

"It is not," Rizpah assured him, waving her hand across the young girl's shoulders. Ares knew it would halt the progress of Ava's long, black wings until he gave the order otherwise and he nodded at the Ker's show of obedience.

"They shall remain beneath the surface, the only knowledge of their existence the two nodes she has discovered already, and I cannot imagine she shall speak of them," Rizpah added, disappearing again.

"She shall not," Ares agreed to the empty space beside him. He held the amulet up again, watching as the jet inside the hematite swirled within as though it held smoke from a fire. It changed from orange, to red, to blue to a grey-black and back again. He smiled, closing his palm around the amulet and wondering just how quickly Ava would prove she was ready for him to appear to her.

31
19th moon full, Skirophorion

Leandros had no clear idea where he would go now that he had returned to Greek shores, though somewhere deep down he had always known he would visit Trachis before going anywhere else. He did not want to bring danger or harm to Ava again; gods knew he had done her enough damage already. He had always caused pain to those he loved – Zita, Skylar, Nasrin, and by extension Alexis, Thaddeus and Hesper. He would not allow it to happen to her.

Without realizing he was doing so, Leandros found he had unwittingly guided Skotos to the hot springs south of Trachis. As he had once before when he had returned from across the waters, one of the horses he had arrived in Delphinium with was left for Archippos and his children. This time it was Raisa, for Nasrin had no need of her where she was now. He had not considered leaving Skotos. Not for a moment. He ran his hand across the stallion's flank and took apples out for each of them.

Leandros knew he should not be as close to the city as he was. But he had not heard from Moeris since he had returned for the first anniversary of Skylar and Alexis' deaths four moons ago. He just needed to know Ava was well, and that she was still in Trachis. If one day she decided to leave, then he would go to her. He would protect her from whatever they faced, and they would not remain in one place, just as he and Skylar never had – until they reached Trachis and Ares found them. He wondered if the situation between Ava and Agrias and Melina had improved. He hoped it had, for all their sakes, though part of him selfishly wished it had not and that Ava would attempt to find him as she grew. Sometimes he missed her so much it hurt.

He shook his head and, leaning against the laurel trees where Skylar and Alexis' ashes were buried, he vowed to them that he would keep his distance, to remain out of Ava's life so she remained safe. Ares had not spoken true when he said she was the Chosen One and Leandros would never have to tell her what her mother was part of, what Zita had been. Her place was in Trachis.

He pushed off the trunk as the last rays of Helios' sun dipped behind the mountain to the west of Trachis. He would visit Moeris and then he would go north to Konitsa. It was time he was reunited with his Thracian kin. They would not ask questions until he was ready and he would not speak of it until they asked. It was best he left the south and all he had lost there.

Leandros lay his hand across Moeris' mouth, the other man jerking awake with the pressure, sword immediately in his hand. Leandros pressed a finger to his own lips and motioned with his head for Moeris to follow him outside. Moeris nodded and Leandros released him.

"What are you doing here? Are you well? Where is Nasrin?" Moeris whispered urgently, joining Leandros in the training square and embracing the taller man.

"I am well. Nasrin is not with me. How are you?" he replied, clapping Moeris on the back and pushing aside the sudden pang of grief his lover's name caused.

"Fine."

"Ava?"

Moeris shrugged. "She is more withdrawn than when we last spoke. She remains at Ophelos and Aspasia's when it suits her, though I have often found her sleeping at the hot springs or here in my quarters at the barracks. She constantly challenges my men and the other young boys who are destined to join us here one day to spar with her. Nikomachos and she believe they spar in secret early in the mornings, but I watch them. Sometimes I have seen her alone, running through the training arena Skylar created."

"Is she proficient with a weapon?" Leandros asked, uncertain he wanted the answer.

Moeris hesitated then gave a curt nod. "A natural, just as you described Skylar to be. Moons ago, she asked me to allow her to join the army. When Sander and Kleitos returned from Persia, her want only grew. I told her I would not – after all she is only ten winters old."

Leandros nodded in return, though it was more to himself than the other man. "And the king and queen? They have not been able to repair the distance between themselves and Ava?" he asked.

"No. Melina is almost as withdrawn as her granddaughter. Ava's wish to join the army does not assist in making repairs," Moeris replied.

Leandros removed the second sheath he wore at his waist, looking it over with sadness and resolution before he raised his eyes to Moeris'. "I am sorry to hear of it. I miss their friendship, as I miss yours."

"I miss you also. Agrias shall be sorry he did not see you. He and Melina are in Macedonia – his brother, King Amycus – passed into the Underworld and there is much he must deal with whilst he mourns him."

"Ava did not go with them?"

"No. She refused, though I cannot speak as to where she slumbers this night," Moeris replied, his curiosity evident at the sword in Leandros' hand.

Leandros drew in a deep breath and blew it all the way out before he spoke again. "This was Skylar's," he said, holding the weapon out to the commander. "If Ava decides that the path of a warrior is for her, and she joins the ranks as an ephebe here in Trachis, gift her with this. She should have it."

"Are you certain? You do not wish me to attempt to talk her out of joining us?"

"If she is anything akin to Skylar, you shall not be able to. Guide her. Teach her how to protect herself, and others, so she does not die in her first battle. It is what Skylar would have wanted. It is what she would have taught her."

Moeris hesitated before taking the sheath and tying the belt at his waist, his hand resting on the pommel of the sword. He nodded to Leandros. "I shall ensure she receives it if the time comes. If she decides otherwise, I shall gift it to her anyway."

"Thank you," Leandros said, taking Moeris in another quick embrace. "There is one more favor I must ask of you."

"Of course."

"Never allow her to know it was Ares who was here the night her mothers were killed."

"Why? Is it not better that she knows the truth, rather than hating the Persians?"

"The Persians are no friends, but she shall want to know why he was here and that is not a tale I wish her to know. Not yet. Perhaps not ever."

Moeris blew out a deep breath. "She shall never hear it from me," he agreed.

"Thank you," Leandros said.

"Where shall you go now?"

"North," Leandros replied. "To Konitsa."

Moeris nodded, knowing Nasrin had been there before she returned to Trachis with Leandros many winters ago, but he did not ask anything further.

"Take care and keep in touch. You know where your messengers can find me."

"I do," Leandros agreed, watching as Moeris returned to the barracks.

Leandros collected Skotos from where he had left him wandering on the plain beneath the north balcony and headed into Trachis itself. He already knew Ava was not at the hot springs, but when he entered his old room at Ophelos', she was not there either. Belatedly he wondered if she was at the palace – with Agrias and Melina not there, perhaps she was.

He doubled back, but could not bring himself to enter the walls where so much still haunted him. Instead, he led Skotos to the south side, tall enough to peek in the high window of the room that had been hers since she was born. Her face was illuminated by the moon outside, the rest of the room in shadow. Her bedclothes were tangled around her body, her dark hair spread across her pillow as she slept, reminding Leandros of Skylar and the many nights he had watched her sleep in a similar position.

"Sleep well, my darling. We shall see each other again one day," he whispered. Ava did not stir, but he smiled sadly as he turned from the window and mounted Skotos, directing him towards the town again and the rivers beyond to the north.

*

Leandros frowned at Skotos' sudden loss of power. He pulled on the reins and the horse skidded to a halt.

"What is it, Boy?" he asked, feeling the clattering heartbeat beneath his hand. Skotos shook his head, whinnying before he dropped to the ground; his heart no longer pounding when Leandros pressed his palm to his stomach. He dropped his head until his forehead rested against the steed's still-warm flesh. "I am sorry," he whispered, tears coursing down his face.

He had pushed Skotos too hard, he was in no doubt of that. He had not meant to but in his haste to leave Trachis far behind, he had not allowed Skotos the rest he required as they travelled north. They had ridden non-stop for almost three days; the constant pace obviously too much for the old horse.

He was still a long way from Konitsa and now Leandros did not know whether to continue north, or to remain nearby. *Is Skotos' death a warning?* he wondered. *What danger am I taking to my friends at Konitsa if I continue to them?* The last time Leandros had been in Konitsa, Nasrin's daughter was killed by men who followed him into their encampment. He could not do that to Theron and Irina again any more than he would place Ava in harm's way. He sat on the hard ground, head in hands as he mourned yet another death he had caused, torn at what he should do.

His answer came the following day. He had almost finished burying Skotos in the hardening ground near the West Macedonian border when a group of herders came along the path.

"May we aid you?" the eldest of the men asked.

Leandros drew his arm across his wet brow. His fingernails were broken and bloodied, not to mention black from the earth. "It is not necessary," he replied, though he did not object as several of the herders set their sticks aside and drew the dark soil over Skotos' cold body.

Their accompanying sheep remained nearby, nibbling at the grass and falling into line again at a signal from their masters. "Where are you headed?" the man asked.

Leandros shrugged. "I have no home, no family."

"We could do with another pair of hands, we lost one of our own this past winter and we are late getting our sheep into the mountains before the full force of summer is upon us. I am Casaereo," he added, holding out his arm.

Leandros hesitated before taking it and squeezing in greeting. "Leandros," he replied. "Perhaps it is time for a change," he murmured.

"A change can be a good thing," Casaereo agreed.

"Sometimes," Leandros nodded. Resting his hand on the pommel of his sword, Leandros considered Casaereo's offer. It was not as if he had a better option, and spending the summer in the mountains would ensure he kept far from Trachis and Konitsa.

I am a danger to those I love. I am not worthy of their company. It is best if I leave Trachis and everyone there far behind. It is best if I allow Ava to remain. They are her people now and she belongs to them. The thoughts struck Leandros with finality and he felt the truth of them through every part of his being.

"I would be honored to join you," he finally said, nodding to Casaereo.

"Good. Shall we continue on now?"

"Yes," Leandros replied, untying his javelin and jamming it into the ground beside Skotos' grave.

Hidden from those before him, Ares grinned, his wish for Leandros to leave Trachis – and remain far away – had finally come to fruition and the God of War would now be free to shape his Chosen One as he wished. When the time came, he knew Ava would not forgive her grandfather easily for deserting her. All would be as he planned. He smirked and disappeared again.

Casaereo handed Leandros a stick, demonstrating how it could be used to assist in walking, and keeping the animals on the narrowing path.

"Perhaps you could begin with four or five sheep?" Casaereo suggested. Leandros only nodded in reply, content to take charge as of many or as few as Casaereo trusted him with.

32
AVA
Trachis
Two winters later
New moon, Moon of Skirophorion, 496BC

And with the new moon, we welcome our new ephebes. They join our ranks in the Army of Thermopylae. For winters now we have been known not just as soldiers from the city we hail from – Trachis – but as the army who protects all of our lands, and we should be feared by those who would seek to take it from us," Moeris announced.

"Opa!" I shouted, my voice joining with the other ephebes and the gathered crowd in the training area of the barracks who had come to see our induction.

The morning was warm, Helios' bright light shining down onto us – a welcome relief after the cooler moons of winter. I stood side by side with the men, wishing I had inherited some of Mumma Skylar's height so it was not so obvious that the other recruits were six winters older than my twelve.

I had begged Moeris to allow me to prove myself against those who would be considered for the army this spring and eventually, after moons of pestering him, he had agreed. I knew the training course by heart, knew the endurance and accuracy needed to pass successfully and I had run and lifted heavy branches to build up my muscles – just as I had seen the boys do. I knew I was ready. I had just needed Moeris to know it.

Leaving Ophelos and Aspasia's home had been easy, finding a place to sleep in Moeris' small room of the barracks, quite another. I knew he feared my grandfather would be angry with him when he learned where I was, though I had heard his reasoning when Agrias came late one night; Moeris had insisted it was better that I remain there where he could ensure I was safe and had food to eat, rather than either of them worrying about me and compromising their own duties. Agrias had reluctantly agreed, and it was then that Moeris began to train me personally.

He told me he could not guarantee I would be allowed into the army, though I knew he had the ear of the men, and if his recommendation was favorable, then they would allow it. And they had, most of them having served under Moeris and Mumma Skylar for many winters. They welcomed me without hesitation, no matter that I was a girl, or too young to be amongst them.

Moeris held his hand up for silence, and the crowd obeyed. "We invite you to join us here at the barracks for a celebratory feast before our new ephebes show you why they were chosen for our great city."

The townsmen stepped forward, gripping arms and slapping us on the back. Lysistratos stood next to me, his grin as wide as mine at being accepted. Before training had begun for places at the barracks, it had been almost two winters since we had seen each other. When Nikomachos and I used to spar early each morning, he sometimes joined us, but after a while it became too hard for me to see them so often – they were too much a reminder of what, or rather who, I had lost and I began to train alone. Lysistratos and Nikomachos were men now, muscled and with the hint of hair on their chins and chests. They certainly no longer resembled the gangly twelve winter old boys who had been two of my closest friends the day Tritonos died on the plain.

"Congratulations," he said.

"And to you," I replied, taking his outstretched arm.

We had seen each other from afar the past moon or so, but had not spoken. I knew he wanted to, and today I felt I was ready. I was happy for the first time in a long time and to share it with Lysistratos felt somehow right.

"Have you seen Nikomachos?" he asked. I shook my head as we released one another. "Neither have I. It is strange for he was accepted just as we were."

"Perhaps he overslept," I replied, though I did not believe that any of the new ephebes would have; I for one had barely slept the night before.

"We were supposed to meet outside the barracks before dawn, but when he did not come, I went to his grandparents' house in town. He was not there either. Pamphilos was gone as well. I searched the agora, but it is if they have simply disappeared," Lysistratos continued.

I frowned. I did not know what would keep Nikomachos from being with us – not when he had trained so fiercely to become a soldier. After our parents died, he spoke with the same determination to avenge them that I did. Winters may have passed, but he not being with us today did not make sense. I could not imagine he would have pushed aside his want to fight the Persians and chosen another path. I had no answers to give, so I simply shrugged in reply.

"He spoke words of joy that the three of us would be reunited," Lysistratos murmured. "It shall be as old times when we used to spar by the Melas River or ride our horses on the plain."

My frown deepened. "It can never be as it was."

Lysistratos shook his head, his eyes never leaving mine as he spoke. "No. But we can forge new paths and make new memories together and they shall be happy again."

"Perhaps," I murmured.

"You have not visited Eumelia for winters," he said, his head to the side ever so slightly.

I swallowed. After Thaddeus and Hesper's deaths, Eumelia had gone to live with Lysistratos' family. The two of them were to be married next winter when Eumelia was thirteen winters. It had been agreed that she would remain in their home until then, her brothers – Nikomachos and Pamphilos – taken in by Hesper's parents nearby. I had not seen her since.

"No," I confirmed. "She is well?"

"She misses you. We were all so close once."

"As I said, it shall never be as it was. Besides, soldiers cannot have friends."

"I do not agree," Lysistratos countered. "We all require the love and support of those both inside and outside the barracks. You do not believe you and I shall become close friends once again?"

"We are to be soldiers," I shrugged. "I imagine our bond shall be closer than friendship. However I do not need anyone outside the barracks to care for me."

Lysistratos considered my words for a long moment, finally shrugging. "You should visit Eumelia. Come to our betrothal. It would mean a lot to her."

"If I am not on assignment, I shall be there," I told him, uncertain I could make such a promise. Uncertain I wanted to.

"Ava," said a once-familiar voice. I stiffened.

"I shall see you inside," Lysistratos muttered, bowing slightly to the man behind me before making his way to the feast.

I turned to face King Agrias. I held his gaze, my jaw clenched tight as he looked me over; girdle about my middle, new sandals shining in the early morning sun. I did not yet wear armor, shield or sword, though I did not expect it to be long before all of them covered my tunic. Moeris already allowed me a shield and sword when we trained together.

"Grandfather," I replied with a nod.

He offered his arm. I hesitated then took it. Taking me by surprise, he pulled me into his arms, hugging me tightly. When I recovered from the shock, I placed my arms around his waist lightly, so many memories crashing down onto me. I swallowed back the tears, holding tight to my anger with him and Melina, the Persians, and the murder of my mothers.

"You are certain this is what you wish for?" he whispered.

"More than anything," I replied, pushing away from him.

He allowed me to break the embrace, sadness etched across his features as he nodded. "Ava," he began, pausing after the single word. "I ..."

"There are no words that need to be spoken between us, King Agrias. As a soldier in your army I shall serve you and our town with loyalty and fierce pride for as many days as I find myself in this world. Any orders or assignments you have for me can find me through Moeris." I would not allow his presence today to cloud the anger I held for him for Papou's banishment. He should suffer just as I had.

"Very well," he said, inclining his head after a moment. "I wish you well in the training display after the feast."

"Thank you," I replied, bowing low.

Agrias took three steps before halting. He turned back, though he kept his eyes on the ground as he spoke. "You shall make them proud. You shall make us all proud." He lifted his gaze then and I held it.

"Was there ever any doubt?" I challenged, lifting my chin defiantly.

"No," he acknowledged, turning on his heel and heading back towards the walkway into the palace rather than the feast.

I blew out a deep breath, glad Agrias had come so he could finally see that I did not need him. That I did not need either of them. I would be a soldier and he and Melina would have to find another heir to their throne, for that title would never be mine again.

"The king is not staying for the exhibition?" Moeris asked as he approached.

"No," I replied simply.

He merely nodded in return. "Come then, I have something for you before the feast."

"What?"

He just smiled and led me to his room. From beside the door, he took a sheathed sword and handed it to me. "This belonged to your Mumma. It is time you had it."

I swallowed around the sudden lump in my throat, aggravated that I felt so much on this day. I had not cried, nor wished for them in a long time. I had put all my energy into making the ephebes. I would not show any weakness now.

I drew the sword from its holder. It was just as I remembered – sharpened wickedly on each side of the blade, an imposing point at one end and the middle shaped as a leaf, wider than the tip and where it joined the handle. It was a simple design, though I knew it had served Mumma well on so many occasions. Except the night she had really needed it. It had been useless then as the Persians attacked. For all her skill and want to protect those she loved, she had been unable to.

"Thank you," I murmured.

"You shall need to start out with wooden training weapons, just as the other new recruits are. It would not do for me to show you such favors. When you have proved you have earned a sword, you may tie this one at your waist and become familiar enough with it to call it your own." I nodded, returning the weapon to its holder. "Now go, eat, you have soldiers and men of the town to impress with your skills," he grinned, giving my shoulder a push.

I smiled in return, placing the sword beneath my bed and heading to the feast. I piled my plate high with food and joined Lysistratos on a klinai, allowing the sounds of the banquet to block out any other thoughts.

33
Three winters later
5th rising, Moon of Skirophorion, 493BC

Ares watched the king of Persia as he breezed through his palace, yelling at anyone who appeared not to be carrying out their given tasks or who simply got in his way, his hand finding unsuspecting cheeks or heads often.

Darius had just received word from his brother, Artaphernes, that the final rebellion had been put to rest – the entirety of Asia Minor was back firmly under his rule once again. It had dragged on too long, and his army was tired, as was he, for it had cost him much.

Losing Sardis in the beginning had been a major blow, but his men had made sure the soldiers from Miletus, the Ionians, and the Greeks who supported them paid dearly. They found their trails and followed them, catching them just outside Ephesus. The Persian cavalry had routed the enemy in quick succession, and though it had taken several more winters, both Aristagoras and Histiaeus were also punished for what they helped incite – both men now in the Underworld.

Ares followed the Great King to his room, whispering words Darius never knew came from the lips of a Greek god. *With matters now settled in Persia, the Greeks must be punished for their support of the revolt. They have undermined the stability of my rule. They have to pay.*

Darius grinned. "It is time Mardonius sailed west and gathered information on the Greeks," he murmured. "First I shall crush Athens and Eretria for their involvement, then I shall conquer the rest of Greece. I shall rule both the east and the west, and no one shall even *think* to rebel against my rule ever again."

ACKNOWLEDGEMENTS

First of all to you the reader … I'm sorry. I know this book was hard, and yes I'll admit it unashamedly: I cried too. This was the hardest one to write because I knew what had to happen. Books 5 and 6 were actually the first ones I wrote for the series and they (and the end of the series) don't work unless what happened here happens. So again, I'm sorry. But please stay with me on this journey in Thermopylae and I hope our new hero will win your heart and you'll forgive me a little for what I had to do.

To my editor Kristie – this one gave us some new challenges with the multiple points of view, and I guess the fans will tell us if we pulled it off or not!

To my wife Renee and daughter Ava, thank you for allowing me the time to disappear into the study for hours on end, I couldn't do what I do if the two of you weren't so supportive.

Thank you also to Graeme who again created an amazing front cover which I hope conveys the feel of the book while also being visually pleasing! I'm sure you'll be glad when the series finishes!

Don't forget that you can connect with me via email at: belinda@belindaharrison.com or online on Instagram at: belindagharrison on Twitter at: beharrison78 on Facebook at: Belinda Harrison Author or through my website at www.belindaharrison.com where I will soon have a merchandise section open for business.

BOOK FIVE OF THE THERMOPYLAE BOUND SERIES *FAR FROM THERMOPYLAE* IS OUT NOW.

ABOUT THE AUTHOR

Belinda Harrison was born and raised in a country town in North East Victoria, Australia. She spent some time experiencing 'big city life' in Melbourne and Sydney in her twenties where she held jobs in a packaging company, an online gaming firm, various temp positions and a hair loss treatment center before the lure of the country recalled her.

She joined her family's business in the world of retail plumbing and appliance sales – which is when she started writing the Thermopylae Bound Series before deciding to leave the familiar and join another well respected local firm in the Real Estate sector where she worked in Commercial Property Management.

Belinda then decided it was time for another change and moved across the road to the local newspaper where she looks after Circulation, writing after hours and around family commitments (and book club).

She currently lives in 'the best part of Victoria' with her wife Renee, daughter Ava, Charlie the dog, and cats Caesar and Max.